The Cat of Christmas Past

by

Kathi Daley

This book is a work of fiction. Names, characters, places, and incidents either are products of the author's imagination or are used fictitiously. Any resemblance to actual events or locales or persons, living or dead, is entirely coincidental.

Copyright © 2015 by Katherine Daley

Version 1.0

Chapter 1

Wednesday, December 9

Holiday music blared through overhead speakers as I, Caitlin Hart, worked with the group of kids from St. Patrick's Catholic Church to decorate the choir room with red and green accents for the upcoming holiday. The children had all agreed to show up early for the regularly scheduled rehearsal for *Away in a Manger*, the Christmas play I had written with my totally wonderful boyfriend, Cody West, for the annual church pageant.

"We need more glue," Trinity Paulson informed me as I hung colorful wreaths on the wall.

"I gave Serenity a whole bottle."

"I know, but it's gone. It had a drippy top and a lot of it got on the table."

Fantastic.

"Why don't you and your sister start on the windows?" I instructed the eight-year-old. "And be careful with the paint. We don't want to get any on the floor."

"Okay."

I stood back and admired our handiwork after Trinity walked away. The room really was beginning to look festive, and in spite of the glue on the table, the red and green construction paper chain the Paulson girls had been working on really did look nice draped around the piano. I was proud of the girls I was beginning to think of as honorary little sisters. Although I'd known the girls their whole lives, I'd recently gotten to know them a lot more intimately, now that their seventeen-year-old sister, Destiny, was working at Coffee Cat Books, the coffee bar/bookstore/cat lounge I owned with my best friend, Tara O'Brian.

"The ornaments aren't balls. They're to go on the tree," I scolded the group of boys who were tossing the small glass balls between themselves.

Whoever had said the more hands at work the quicker the task had never worked with twenty-three kids aged six to fourteen.

"Ricky started it," six-year-old Robby Davey tattled.

"Well, I'm ending it."

God, I sound like my mother.

When I asked everyone to show up early to help with the chore, I'd figured Cody would be here to help me supervise, but he'd gotten held up working on an article for the *Madrona Island News*, the local newspaper he owns and publishes. He'd called earlier to say that he wouldn't be able to make it to the church until just prior to the rehearsal.

"Can I put the angel on the top of the tree, Ms. Cait?" six-year-old Stephanie Collins asked.

"I'm sorry, Steph," I answered the girl with the long dark ringlets, "but Christy already asked me if she could do it after Mass last Sunday."

"Christy isn't here," Stephanie pointed out.

I looked around the room for the thirteen-year-old. Stephanie was right; Christy hadn't shown up as planned. I frowned. I hoped she was okay. She'd been so excited about the decorating party and she was thrilled that it was her turn to play Mary in the pageant.

"Does anyone know why Christy isn't here?" I asked the room at large.

"Her mom got a letter," Holly Carter answered. "My mom got one too."

"A letter?" I asked.

"Everyone living in the Bayview Apartments needs to move before the end of the month," Matthew Wildwood informed me.

"What? Why?"

"The old guy who owns the building is kicking everyone out," Matthew, who was the oldest choir member at fourteen, answered.

"Kicking everyone out? Why on earth would he do that?"

Matthew shrugged. "I'm not sure, but my grandma called my mom and told her that she was going to be homeless. My mom said she could move into my room and I could move in with my little brother, but I'm not sure Grandma is real happy about that, and I know I'm not happy about it. I'm a teenager. I need my space. If Grandma moves in with us we'll all be miserable."

"I think that's the point," twelve-year-old Holly informed me. "My mom said the guy who owns the apartment building is nothing more than a mean old man who's so unhappy with his own pathetic life that he actually takes pleasure in ruining the lives of others."

I realized Holly must be talking about Balthazar Pottage, an old recluse who lived on a private island he never left, despite the fact that he owned quite a lot of land in the area. Balthazar was as mean and miserly as he was miserable. I didn't know the entire story, but I did seem to remember that he'd suffered a great tragedy in his past that turned him into the monster most considered him to be.

"My mom said we might have to move off the island if we can't find another affordable place to live," Holly added. "I don't want to move. I like it here. All my friends are here."

The Bayview Apartments were one of the few affordable rental properties on the island. Most of the families who lived in the rundown units were single-income families who had little choice but to deal with leaky faucets and drafty walls that did little to keep out the winter chill. Most considered Pottage to be a slum lord, but few had the means to fight the man who was as wealthy as he was mean.

"If Christy has to move can I be Mary in the play?" Serenity asked.

I looked toward the front of the room, where she and Trinity were painting snowflakes on the choir room window.

"We usually choose one of the older girls," I answered. "I guess if Christy isn't able to do it Noel would be next in line."

"May as well give it to Serenity," thirteen-year-old Noel Holiday answered. "My mom got a letter too. She's going to look for another place we can afford, but with Timmy's medical bills she said we have a snowball's chance in hell of finding one."

I considered admonishing Noel for using the word hell in a church building, but I knew her little brother was battling leukemia and that his medical expenses were the main reason the family, who actually had a decent income, was forced to live in the apartments. I imagined Noel was simply repeating what she'd heard from her overworked and overstressed mother.

"So can I be Mary?" Serenity asked.

"We'll see."

I returned to my task with a heavy heart. I knew there were twelve apartments in the rundown building. In addition to Christy's, Holly's, and Noel's family, and Matthew's grandmother, five of the additional eight apartments were occupied by neighbors who attended St. Patrick's on a weekly basis. Many of the families had lived on the island for more than a generation. If Balthazar Pottage kicked everyone out it was going to affect a whole lot of people I cared about.

I thought about Hazel Keller, an eighty-six-year-old woman who not only served as an active volunteer in the community but was an active member of the church. Where would she go if she were evicted? I knew she didn't have a lot of money, but Madrona Island was her home. It would be tragic to displace her at this point in her life.

And then there was Laverne Sullivan, a retired teacher who'd spent a good portion of the money she'd saved over her life trying to keep up with her husband's medical expenses before he died. Laverne had worked hard and provided a service to the community. In my opinion she deserved to enjoy her retirement surrounded by those whose lives she had affected.

If I remembered correctly there were two other seniors in the building besides Hazel, Laverne, and Matthew's grandma, Rosanna. All, likewise, were long-term members of the community who I'm certain would have no desire to move.

And what about Angel Haven, a newly married friend of mine who was pregnant with her first child?

Where would Angel and Jesse find another place they could afford? Angel was due to deliver any day now, and the thought of the new family being displaced from their home during a time in their lives that should be filled with joy left me unsettled.

"Anabelle won't share the glitter," Robby complained.

"He's just making a mess with it," Annabelle defended herself.

Annabelle was right. Ricky and Robby *were* making a mess with the glitter.

"Robby, why don't you and Ricky start untangling the lights we plan to put on the tree?" I suggested.

"That's boring," Robby complained.

"It's an important job," I persuaded. "No matter how many pretty ornaments we put on the tree it's really the lights that make it come to life."

Robby looked at me like he was trying to figure out if I was attempting to trick him into the unpleasant chore.

"I usually save the lights for my very best helpers," I added.

"Okay." Robby smiled a toothless grin because both of his front teeth were missing. I remembered the Christmas when I was in the first grade; both my front teeth had been missing as well. My brother Danny had made fun of me, but my oldest brother

Aiden, who I worshipped, thought it was cool, so I ran around town sporting my toothless grin proudly.

"Are we going to have a Santa at the church dinner this year?" Ricky asked.

"I'm not sure," I admitted. St. Patrick's held a community dinner and a Christmas fair the Saturday before Christmas every year. I planned to help with the event this year but hadn't heard if a Santa had been procured.

"I hope so, 'cause my mom said she's too busy to take me to the mall in Seattle and I need to talk to Santa about my sneakers."

"Sneakers?"

"I need new shoes. My old ones are too small and they squish my toes. My mom said I could wear my big brother's old ones, but I want sneakers of my own. Blue ones with a racing stripe like Robby has."

I knew Ricky's family struggled to make ends meet and really hoped Ricky would be able to receive the shoes he desired. Maybe I'd talk to Sister Mary about it. She usually organized a drive to buy gifts for families who were having a hard time making ends meet.

"I'll talk to the committee to see if they plan to have Santa come for a visit," I promised. "If they haven't invited him already I'll suggest it."

"Thank you, Ms. Cait. If I'm real good I'm hoping to get new socks to go with the new shoes. My old ones all have holes in the toe."

I smiled at the overactive but very sweet little boy. I planned to make sure he received the shoes and socks he wanted if I had to buy them myself. I'd heard rumors that Ricky's family might be forced to move from the island if his dad couldn't find work. It was getting harder and harder to make a living in the fishing industry and a lot of people whose families had lived on Madrona Island for generations had been forced to move since the cannery closed.

"Sorry I'm late," Cody said as he hurried in through the choir room door after most of the decorations had been hung and placed.

"Have you heard about the Bayview Apartments?" I asked as I brushed snowflakes off his shoulder.

I tried to find comfort in Cody's blue eyes, but all I saw was the same worry I felt. "I have. That's where I was, actually. I spoke to the building manager, Bob Cranwell, who informed me that Mr. Pottage is going to tear the place down right after the first of the year. Everyone needs to be out by the end of the month."

"Why is he tearing it down? And why now, with Christmas just around the corner?"

Cody took off his coat and hung it on the coatrack near the door. "The manager didn't know. All he could tell me was that everyone in the building received a letter informing them that they needed to vacate by December 31."

"Can Pottage do that?" I wondered.

"Unfortunately, he can. According to Mr. Cranwell, everyone is there on a week-to-week agreement. All that legally has to be given is a week's notice, so Pottage seems to think that giving three weeks' notice makes him some kind of a saint."

"That's insane. Where will everyone go?"

"I don't know."

Cody looked troubled. I'd been around him enough to know that he wasn't the sort to be concerned unless there really was something to worry about.

"We have to do something," I announced as Cody continued into the room.

"Like what?" he asked as he approached the piano.

"I don't know, but there's no way I'm going to stand by and let that old miser ruin everyone's Christmas. It seems like a lot of our neighbors are having a hard time of it this year. Tossing twelve families out on the street is going to make things harder for everyone on the island. We're a community and we need to support one another. There must be something we can do."

Cody said a few words to the pair of girls who were sitting at the piano chatting about the new boy at school. They vacated the bench so Cody could sort through the sheet music he kept under the seat.

"Based on what I've been able to find out today," Cody said as he sorted, "we'll need a miracle to change the old man's mind. According to Mr.

Cranwell, he seems pretty determined to follow through with his plan."

"Well, I guess if we need a miracle we're in the right place to ask for one."

I looked around the newly decorated choir room. I knew in my heart that miracles were real and Christmas was the best time to ask for one. In the grand scheme of things the destruction of a single apartment building might not seem like a big deal, but to the twelve families who lived there, it was everything.

"Cait," Trinity said from her place near the window.

"Yes, Trinity?" I tried to smile so the kids wouldn't pick up on my despair.

"There's a big beige and white cat looking in the window at me. I think he wants in. I know animals aren't allowed in the church building, but it's snowing and he looks cold."

I walked across the room and opened the door. In walked a large cat with a collar around its neck. I bent down and looked at the name tag. It read Ebenezer. I smiled as I realized we'd just found the help we'd need to make our miracle happen.

Chapter 2

Thursday, December 10

"Are you sure this is a good idea?" I asked Ebenezer.

My furry companion and I stood in front of the tall wrought-iron gate that secured the house where Balthazar Pottage lived, on the private island he owned. It had already been a long day and the resolve I'd felt earlier that day was beginning to waver. It was cold and windy and snow flurries danced in the air. I would have appreciated the seasonal weather had I not been exhausted after the rough ferry ride to San Juan Island, followed by the extremely frigid private boat ride my brother Danny had arranged for me with his friend Trevor.

Ebenezer squeezed through the opening between the bars, seemingly answering my question.

"Okay, I get the idea that you think we need to do this, but I'm never going to fit through the opening between these bars and the gate is locked. Any ideas?"

"Meow." Ebenezer took off along the tall stone wall that surrounded the property. I could no longer see where he was, but he'd headed east, so I walked in that direction, looking for an opening of some kind.

I'd dressed warmly that morning in a thick turtleneck sweater, heavy jeans, and a down jacket, but with the steady wind the temperature had dropped to the point where even though I was dressed for the weather I was freezing. I hoped Ebenezer actually had a plan and wasn't taking me on a wild-goose chase. I found I much preferred the thought of curling up by the fire in my little oceanside cabin with Cody and my dog Max.

The thought of Cody made me frown. He wasn't going to be happy that I'd come on this little adventure with only a cat for protection. We'd discussed it after we went back to my place the previous evening and agreed that we'd work on the project together. Was it my fault that this pushy cat wanted to visit the old man on the same day Cody was in Seattle covering a story for the newspaper?

Surely he'd understand.

Or maybe not.

The last thing I wanted to do was get into an argument with the man I loved two weeks before Christmas.

I pulled my jacket tighter around my petite frame. It didn't snow often in the islands, and we mostly enjoyed a mild climate, but every now and then a storm blew down from the north and blanketed the area in snow and below-average temperatures. The odds that I'd have cause to head out on a recognizance mission during such a storm were remote, or at least they would be if some unseen force hadn't decided to make me the guardian of the cats Tansy was forever sending my way.

Tansy and her best friend, Bella, are rumored to be witches. Neither of them will confirm or deny their witchy status, but both women know things that can't be empirically explained. Bella and Tansy lived in the touristy village of Pelican Bay, which is located on the southern end of the island. They owned and operated Herbalities, a specialty shop dealing in herbs and fortune telling. While both Bella and Tansy seemed to be more in tune with the natural rhythms of the universe than most, it was Tansy who demonstrated a level of intuition that's downright disturbing.

I'd been pretty sure Ebenezer had been sent by Tansy due to the perfect timing of his arrival at the church, but when I'd gotten back to my cabin last night, she'd called to make certain he'd arrived safely, confirming my suspicion. I tried to pry additional information out of the taciturn woman, but all she would say was to trust Ebenezer and he would show me the way.

My relationship with Tansy's cats began less than a year ago, when she sent me a large gray cat named Romeo to help out with the investigation of the murder of an island council member. I guess Tansy had decided the cat and I had worked well together because after Romeo left other cats began showing up. Ebenezer was the sixth one I'd worked with in this same capacity, although I worked with other cats every day because I, along with my Aunt Maggie, operate a cat sanctuary that's dedicated to sheltering and rehabilitating the island's feral cat population.

Now that Mayor Bradley was dead the cats might not be in the danger they once were, but that remained to be seen.

"Ebenezer, are you still there?" I called. "Can you hear me?"

I stopped walking and watched as my feline companion squeezed through a small break in the wall. The break wasn't large enough for most adults to squeeze through, but since I'm petite I realized I'd be able to make it without a problem.

The view on the other side of the wall was much like the one on the outside: thick foliage covered with a layer of snow. I couldn't see the house, but I suspected it was in the center of the island, where it would be the most protected from both the elements and intruders.

I could hear waves crashing in the background. I was supposed to call Trevor when I was ready for a ride home, although based on the increase in wind velocity, I wasn't sure he'd be able to make the return trip to pick me up if we didn't hurry.

I followed Ebenezer back to the dirt path that led to the house and then up to the front porch. I could feel my heart pounding as I worked up the courage to knock. I wasn't sure what it was I was afraid of. The man was ancient; surely he wouldn't, or more importantly couldn't, hurt me.

"Last chance to back out," I said as I stood on the cement porch, looking at the thick hardwood door.

"Meow."

"He might not even be here." The house was a large stone structure that looked dark from the outside. Of course most of the windows were covered in thick drapes that would block out the light from inside the house, should there be any.

Ebenezer just looked at me. I could see he was becoming impatient with my stalling.

"Okay," I breathed. "Here goes nothing."

I took a deep breath and knocked on the door. The iron knocker made a deep, hollow sound that seemed to echo through the area. After less than a minute an old man, stooped with age, opened the door.

"Ebenezer." The man looked at the cat. "Wherever had you gotten off to?"

The cat meowed and trotted inside.

"This is your cat?" I asked the emaciated old man.

"It is. Who are you? And what are you doing on my property?"

"My name is Caitlin Hart. I live on Madrona Island. I found Ebenezer last night at St. Patrick's Catholic Church and he led me here today."

The old man, who I assumed to be Balthazar Pottage, turned and looked at the cat, who had jumped onto a table just off to the side and begun to purr.

"Damn cat," the man grumbled, but I noticed there was warmth in his eyes as he picked him up and started down the hall. "Close the door behind you," he instructed.

Was the man inviting me in? He'd told me to close the door behind me, but had he meant come in and then close the door, or simply close the door on my way out? Because he hadn't specified, I decided to take my chances and come in. I closed the door and then followed the man down the hall.

The dark hardwood doors on either side of the hall were all closed. Eventually the man turned into an open room that was cozy in a shabby sort of way. There was a nice fire in the large stone fireplace that seemed to be the only heat supplied to the room. Or the whole house, for that matter. It was almost as cold in the house as it had been outside.

The white-haired man sat down in one of the chairs placed in front of the fireplace. The cat looked quite content as he curled up in his lap. I looked around the room, trying to decide what to do. There was an old sofa, but the distance from the fire was twice that from the chairs, so I decided to sit down across from my host in the other chair.

"Nice house," I said, trying for polite conversation. I noticed a half-eaten bowl of broth on a table next to the chair.

"Bah."

"I take you're Balthazar Pottage?"

"Who wants to know?"

"I told you. My name is Caitlin Hart."

"Why are you here?"

"To return your cat. At least I guess I'm supposed to return him. He showed up at the church last night and then led me here this afternoon."

"Hmph."

I noticed the man didn't seem at all surprised that his cat had been found miles away on another island or that Ebenezer had managed to communicate with me his intent to pay a visit to the house today.

In spite of the fact that I was sitting across from the man he didn't say another word. He just stared hypnotically into the fire, as if I weren't even in the room. How in the heck was I supposed to find a smooth segue into a discussion concerning the Bayview Apartments if he wasn't inclined to speak to me?

"I suppose I should be going, now that Ebenezer is safely home," I began.

The man didn't answer.

"I'm glad I finally had a chance to meet you. I've always wondered about your house. You can't see it from the water with all the trees on the property. I hadn't realized it was so large. From the outside it appears to have three full stories. Is there an attic at the top? It's hard to tell for certain based on the roof line alone."

The man closed his eyes. Was he going to sleep? I knew I was rambling, but I figured it was better to keep talking than to let the conversation die. Even if said conversation had, to this point, been one-sided at best.

"I imagine it gets lonely living here all alone in this big house. I guess it's a good thing you have Ebenezer for company," I continued to babble. "He seems like such an agreeable cat. I really enjoyed my time with him. Still, it's odd he showed up all the way over on Madrona Island. I wonder how he got there."

The man didn't respond.

"I suppose he must have stowed away on one of the boats that brings you supplies. I'm sure you must get deliveries of one sort or another on somewhat of a regular schedule. Food, propane, that sort of thing. Do you travel to the other islands often? I've heard you prefer to remain on your island most of the time."

The man still didn't respond, but he did open his eyes. Maybe he was finally getting tired of my rambling and would be willing to engage in a two-way conversation. "You still here?" Pottage asked, as if to indicate he hadn't heard a word I'd said. Not that

I blamed him. Even I was getting tired of my endless chattering about nothing in particular.

"I'm afraid so. I don't suppose you have a phone? I'm supposed to call my friend when I want him to come pick me up, but the cell service is a bit sketchy."

"Why are you really here?" the man asked.

"I told you, to return your cat."

He sat up straighter. "The cat comes and goes on his own timeline. If he brought you here it was for a reason. I'd like to know what that reason is."

I moved forward in my chair in an attempt to look taller and therefore more formidable. "I wanted to speak to you about the Bayview Apartments."

"What about them?"

"I hear you plan to tear them down."

"So?" The man glared at me.

"So, a lot of really wonderful people live in those apartments. If you tear them down they'll be homeless."

The man sat forward and mimicked my body language. He might be old, but he was at least a foot taller than me, which made him look a tad more threatening than I was comfortable with.

"The apartments have fallen into disrepair. I've been notified that I need to bring them up to code or they'll be condemned. I chose to have them torn down instead, not that it's any of your business."

I adjusted my position in my chair so I was farther away from the man's dark stare. "Why don't you just fix the place up? If you did you'd have a piece of property with increased value and the tenants wouldn't have to move."

The man got up from his chair and slowly made his way across the room. He picked up a piece of paper and then walked back across the room to hand it to me. It was an invoice that I didn't totally understand, though I did understand the large number at the bottom of the paper.

"This is the estimate I was given when I inquired what it would take to bring the place up to the current code," Pottage informed me.

"Wow."

"If I spend this amount of money on that building I'll need to double the rents in order to recover the cost. Not a single person living in the building could afford to have their rent doubled."

"No, I guess not," I admitted.

"The easiest solution to the problem is to tear the place down and sell off the land."

That did make sense from a business standpoint, but certainly not from a human one.

"It might be hard to find a buyer," I tried, even though I knew what I'd said was a bald-faced lie. The apartment building had been built on an oceanfront lot that had to be worth millions today.

"I already have a buyer. He's made me a strong offer. He plans to build condos in the spring."

"So why the rush? Why not wait until the spring to tear down the old apartment building? I'm sure we could work something out with the building inspector to give the tenants more notice."

"The buyer wants the tenants gone and the building removed before he'll sign the final paperwork. He's offered me an incentive to have the building torn down by the end of January."

"You have a lot of money," I pointed out.

"I do."

"Can't you just fix up the place and let the tenants stay?"

"As I said before, to recoup my expenses the rents would need to be so high none of the present tenants could afford them."

I hated to admit it, but the man had a point. A good one. The only reason the people who were in the building lived there was because it was the most affordable rental on the island. If the rents were doubled everyone would have to move anyway.

"I realize it might not be the best business decision, but couldn't you leave the rents the same?" I suggested. "At least for a while, until the people can make other plans."

"Why would I do that?" The man sat back down in the chair, but I noticed that the cat had moved to a place by the fire.

"As an act of human kindness," I said, a question in my voice.

"Bah. Why should I be kind to others when others have never been kind to me?"

I didn't have an answer to that.

I looked around the room, searching frantically for a solution to the seemingly impossible problem before me. Ebenezer got up from his spot and walked over to a nearby table. There was a book on top, which he swatted to the floor. I joined him and picked it up.

"*A Christmas Carol* by Charles Dickens. A classic. Are you reading it?"

"Trying. My eyes aren't what they used to be, I'm afraid."

I opened the book and looked at the title page. There was an inscription there that read: *To my husband on our first Christmas, Love, Belle.*

"You were married?" I asked.

"For a while, a long time ago."

I closed the book and set it back on the table. I started to step away but then changed my mind. I needed a way to get through to the old man, and if prior experience with Tansy's cats was any indication, Ebenezer had knocked the book off the table for a reason.

"I can read to you for a while before I leave if you'd like."

The man looked at me. He appeared to be surprised by my offer.

"Why would you do that?"

I shrugged. "I need to wait for my ride back to San Juan Island. It's almost Christmas and I enjoy the story of Scrooge. I assume you do as well, considering your cat is named Ebenezer."

"I don't need a nursemaid."

"I know," I answered. "I just thought I'd read to pass the time and I'm happy to read out loud as long as I'm at it."

"Do whatever you want," the man grumbled.

I smiled.

I picked up the book and opened it to the first page.

MARLEY was dead: to begin with. There is no doubt whatever about that. The register of his burial was signed by the clergyman, the clerk, the undertaker, and the chief mourner. Scrooge signed it: and Scrooge's name was good upon 'Change, for anything he chose to put his hand to. Old Marley was as dead as a door-nail.

Mind! I don't mean to say that I know, of my own knowledge, what there is particularly dead about a door-nail. I might have been inclined, myself, to regard a coffin-nail as the deadest piece of ironmongery in the trade. But the wisdom of our ancestors is in the simile; and my unhallowed hands shall not disturb it, or the Country's done for. You will therefore permit me to repeat, emphatically, that Marley was as dead as a door-nail.

Scrooge knew he was dead? Of course he did.

I noticed Pottage had closed his eyes as I read. He appeared to be listening to the story rather than sleeping, however. I even noticed a faint smile on his thin lips a time or two. Ebenezer was curled up in his lap, purring loudly as the old man listened to the tale.

After a half hour my phone dinged, indicating that I had a text. Trevor had anticipated that I might have a problem with cell service so he'd come back for me and was waiting at the dock. He indicated that the storm was getting worse and we'd need to leave now or risk being trapped on the island.

"I have to go." I closed the book. "My ride is here."

"But you haven't finished the story." The man looked more than just a little disappointed.

"The storm is getting worse. I really need to go," I insisted.

"Will you come back to finish the story?"

I stood up and pulled on my jacket. The trip from Madrona Island was long and not all that pleasant during the winter, but reading to the old man would be a small price to pay if …

"I'll come back on Monday to finish the story if you promise to at least consider an alternative for the

Bayview Apartments that will allow the current residents to stay."

The man nodded his head.

"Then I guess we have a deal."

Chapter 3

Friday, December 11

"That book you ordered came in," Tara informed me as we worked side by side to unpack and catalogue the shipment of merchandise we'd just received for our store.

"Oh, good. I plan to take it with me when I visit Balthazar Pottage on Monday."

Tara stopped what she was doing and looked up at me. "Are you still determined to get the old man to rescind the eviction letters to the tenants of the Bayview Apartments?"

I shrugged. "I'm going to try. I know it's a long shot, but I figure I'll have his undivided attention for several hours when I go back. Once I finish the book, I'm going to insist we talk about the apartments."

"And you actually think he'll consider remodeling the apartments at his own expense even though it's unlikely he'll ever recover his investment?"

"He might," I said with more certainty than I felt. "Apparently, Pottage likes to read and has been unable to do so since his eyesight began to fail. I'm going to use that to my advantage and volunteer to go out to the island to read to him every week if he'll save the apartment building. He doesn't need the money. Based on everything I've heard, he has a ton of it. Being able to have his favorite books read to him might be worth the cost to repair the building to him."

Tara stopped what she was doing. She turned and looked at me. "You know, there are books on tape."

"Of course I know that, but I don't plan to mention it to him. Besides, in spite of his gruff exterior I think he appreciates the company. Even if he prefers to keep his own company most of the time, it must get lonely living out there on that island all by himself. He doesn't even have a television. I really can't imagine what he does to pass the time."

Tara returned to her task. "Are you sure it isn't dangerous? I mean, he does have a reputation for being disagreeable and he does live alone on an isolated island."

"He's like a hundred years old. I think I can take him if it comes down to a fight." I laughed.

"Unless he has a gun," Tara pointed out.

I began stacking the empty boxes. The store had gotten a lot busier with the approaching holiday and restocking the shelves had become a regular occurrence.

"I don't think he's dangerous," I informed Tara. "I had Cody do a background search on him last night just to be sure. He's really good at digging up any information he needs for stories, so I figured finding out the details of Pottage's past wouldn't be all that hard for him. Based on what Cody found out, I think he's just a bitter old man who's chosen to shut out the world."

"Do you know why he's so bitter?"

"Actually, I think I do. I saw an inscription in the book I was reading to him from a woman named Belle. I asked him about her and he said he was married a long time ago. I've since found out that his relationship with Belle ended quite tragically."

Tara began unpacking the new shipment of pink Coffee Cat Books mugs. "Tragically how?"

I sat back and looked at Tara. "For the story to be truly appreciated I need to back up a bit and start from the beginning."

"Okay, I'm game. So where's the beginning?"

I could see I had Tara's complete attention, and her complete impatience as well. I pushed the box I'd been working on aside and started the next as I began my tale.

"Cody found out that Balthazar Pottage was orphaned at an early age. He didn't have all the details, but he thought he was around five. After his parents died he lived in a children's home, which, it seemed from what Cody could find, wasn't a pleasant place to grow up."

"Some of those places are pretty nice these days," Tara pointed out.

"True, but that was a long time ago, and it seems the home he lived in was known for its rigid structure and severe discipline policy. Anyway, when he was old enough to be on his own he got a job and began to save his money. In just a few years he bought his first business, and from that point forward he began to build a financial empire. By the time he was in his midfifties he was still single but had amassed a fortune."

"I'm assuming this is where Belle comes into the picture," Tara commented as she sat back and waited for me to continue.

"It is. She was the daughter of a man whose business he'd bought out of bankruptcy. At the time she was thirty-two to his fifty-six, but they fell in love and married. Or at least I know they married. I can only imagine that they fell in love. Anyway, Pottage built her a grand home on the north end of Madrona Island."

"They lived here?" Tara asked.

"Part of the time. Cody discovered they had homes both on Madrona Island and in Seattle. It seemed as if Belle spent a lot of her time on the island, at least during the final year of the marriage."

"Are you referring to that old mansion on the point that's been deserted as far back as I can remember?" Tara asked.

"Yes. That was the home Pottage built for Belle. He abandoned it after."

"After what?"

"Hang on, I'm getting to it." I moved over to the coffee bar and began assembling what we'd need for the rush when the next ferry arrived.

"Anyway," I continued, "Pottage built Belle a grand home and three years after they wed they had a son: Charles. Twenty years ago, when Charles was just six weeks old, he was kidnapped from his crib during a reception the family hosted on Christmas Eve to celebrate his christening."

"Oh, God." Tara paled.

"No one ever did figure out what happened to him. Initially the police believed Pottage would receive a ransom note, but he never did. And I'm afraid the story gets worse."

"Worse how?"

"Five days after her son disappeared Belle was killed in an auto accident. It seems her car slid on the ice just a mile from her home and she was killed instantly."

Tara cringed. "That poor man. No wonder he retreated from the world."

"Yeah. I had very little respect for the mean old man, but now I have nothing but compassion. I guess you never know what's really behind a person's behavior until you walk in their shoes."

I returned to the box I had been unpacking, Tara went back to her task, and we worked side by side in silence. Balthazar Pottage's story was a tragic one that couldn't help but put a damper on the holiday spirit we'd been enjoying prior to my sharing the sad little tale. I really couldn't imagine living with the loss of a spouse and a son in such tragic ways.

"Is Destiny coming in today?" I asked in an attempt to change the subject and, hopefully, lighten the mood a bit.

"She's at the church doing her final exams for the semester. She wants to be done with her schoolwork before the baby comes, so she's putting in extra time now. I don't think we should count on her to be able to work here much if at all for the next month or two. Besides the schoolwork, she's gotten to the point in her pregnancy where she really should be taking it easy. I think we'll be fine in the long run, but I'm a little worried about keeping up with everything between now and Christmas."

"Maybe we should hire some temporary help."

"That might be a good idea. I'm just not sure if we can find someone who wants a job for just two weeks."

"I imagine most people in the job market are looking for something a bit more long term," I agreed.

"I suppose we could post a notice in the window to see if anyone's interested," Tara suggested. "Maybe we'll find someone who simply wants a little extra cash for the holiday and doesn't mind the temporary nature of the job."

"It couldn't hurt to put it out there and see what happens," I agreed. I set the box I'd been working on aside and started on the next one, which contained a selection of holiday pens and colorful journals. "Has Destiny made up her mind about keeping the baby?"

"Not as far as I know," Tara answered. "She refused to finalize the agreement with the adoption agency, but when I asked her about a shower, she said she probably wouldn't be needing any baby things. I can see she's really struggling with the whole thing. In my opinion she probably won't make up her mind until after the baby is born."

Although Destiny had just turned seventeen and the baby's father wasn't in the picture at all, I felt like she had the support she would need to make a go of it should she decide to keep the baby. Living with Tara seemed to be working out for both of them, and Destiny had done an excellent job as an employee of the store. We planned to keep her on as a full-time employee for as long as she wanted the job. On the other hand, she was a bright girl who could do well in college and could probably pursue any type of career she wanted, though with a baby to care for a college degree probably wouldn't be in the picture, at least for a while. Destiny's decision to keep her baby or not would most likely define the direction her life would take from that point forward, so I could understand her need to think it through very carefully.

I could see the ferry nearing the island. It would be docking within the next few minutes. One of the things I loved the most about the location of our shop was that it provided a perfect viewpoint from which to watch the boats as they made their way into and out of the harbor.

"Are you going to the Christmas fair and spaghetti dinner the church is sponsoring next weekend?" Tara asked me as the ferry began its approach.

I nodded. "I volunteered to help with the dinner, and it looks like I'm now in charge of finding a Santa for the event. I thought I'd ask Cody to do it if he isn't too busy."

"Seems like he has been lately. Busy, that is."

"Yeah. I guess I could ask Danny, but I don't see him being all that good with little kids. I'm not even sure he's going. It seems like he's had a lot on his mind lately."

"I've noticed that as well," Tara confirmed. "I mentioned getting a new dress for the event and he mumbled something about maybe having plans. I'm not sure I'm even going to go."

"You should definitely go and you should absolutely get a new dress. Don't let grumpy old Danny ruin your fun. A new dress is part of the fun. I loved getting all dressed up for the fair even as a child."

"I still remember that red velvet dress you had, with the black faux fur jacket," Tara commented. "I was so jealous."

"My mom made that dress. I'm pretty sure she still has it up in the attic. She saved boxes of things from our childhood, assuring us that we'd want them for our own children someday."

"She's probably right. You most likely will end up glad your mom saved all your old stuff. My mom isn't sentimental at all. I don't think she saved a single item from my childhood."

I shrugged. "I guess people approach memory keeping differently. She has a bunch of photos of you on her wall."

"Yeah, I guess. Still, it would have been nice to know I had family heirlooms to pass on to my own daughter, should I have one."

The bell over the door tinkled as a woman in a red coat came into the store.

"Excuse me," the woman began, "I'm looking for a book, but I can't remember either the title or the author. Can you help me?"

"We can try," Tara offered. "What do you know about it?"

"It's a mystery set at Christmas," the woman said. "There's a teacher who dies and an animal rescue worker who tries to solve the case."

"I think I know the book you're looking for. The book is called *Christmas Cozy* and it was written by one of our most popular authors. Follow me and I'll show you to the right shelf."

Tara led the woman across the store. It appeared she'd guessed correctly because the two women entered into a lengthy conversation about the book. It seemed the woman wanted to buy a dozen copies to use as gifts for the members of her book club.

I turned my attention back to the inventory we'd been shelving. I love the holidays, when there are so many fun and imaginative items to display. Tara had changed the window display a dozen times since Thanksgiving, but she seemed to be having fun with the ever-evolving project.

I watched as the ferry approached the dock. "White Christmas" was playing softly on the loudspeaker, and I realized we might actually have one this year. It had been snowing gently off and on all day. It really wasn't accumulating on the ground, but it looked pretty fluttering around in the sky. I stood at the window and looked out toward the harbor. Many of the boats had been dry docked for the winter, but there were a few hearty souls, like my brother Danny, who lived in their boats year-round. Of course he bunked at Aunt Maggie's house during the worst storms, but he didn't seem to mind the dark and dreary days we often experienced during the winter.

"Did you get the lady all taken care of?" I asked Tara after the customer left the store.

"Yeah, she wanted a dozen copies and we only have three in stock, but she doesn't need them until next week so I'll special order them. Did you get the coffee bar ready for the crowd?"

"I did. I noticed we were getting low on the syrup for both the gingerbread lattes and the peppermint mochas. Maybe I'll order some more."

"Okay, but don't over order," Tara cautioned. "Once Christmas has passed requests for those specialty drinks is bound to decrease dramatically."

"I'll just make a note of what we're low on. I'll leave it to you to decide what to order."

I turned back toward the coffee bar.

"Would you look at that?" Tara murmured as I started a fresh pot of coffee.

"Look at what?"

"It looks like you have a visitor."

I walked over to the window and looked toward the ferry, which had just begun to unload the walk-on passengers. Ebenezer was trotting down the walkway with a tall, dark-haired young man who looked to be in his twenties following him. Ebenezer darted across the road and came directly to our door. I opened it and he trotted inside.

"Is this your cat?" the man asked after I invited him to come inside.

"No, but he likes to visit," I answered.

"I saw him on the ferry. He appeared to be alone, so I've been keeping an eye on him. He sure is a friendly cat. I was afraid he was a stray."

"Ebenezer is a very independent cat, but thank you for watching out for him. Can I offer you a coffee or other hot beverage? My treat."

"A coffee would be great," the man answered. "My name is Alex Turner, by the way."

"I'm Cait," I said as I handed him his coffee. "Are you visiting the island for the day?"

"Actually, I'm here to look for a temporary job. I attend the university in Portland, but I really want to spend my break on the island. I have a place to stay, but I'll need spending money."

"You don't have family on the mainland you want to spend your break with?"

"No. Not anymore. My dad passed away when I was a baby and my mother just passed recently."

"I'm so sorry."

The man shrugged. "It's been tough since Mom died. I think a change of scenery for the holiday will be good for me. This is delicious coffee, by the way."

"Thank you. It's our own special blend." I glanced at Tara, who was busy with customers. "We might have a temp job available for the next couple of weeks. I'll need to talk to my partner when it slows down a bit. If you want to either wait until the store clears out or come back in a little while, I can talk to you about it some more."

Alex looked toward the cat lounge. "Is it okay to wait in there?"

"Absolutely. Take Ebenezer with you, but be sure he stays away from Lucy. She is our newest feline and she's still a little edgy around new cats."

"My mom's name was Lucy. She had a tendency to be edgy around strangers as well." Alex laughed.

I smiled and then returned to my job. I spent the next twenty minutes making coffee drinks and ringing up purchases for the dozen customers who had come in from the ferry. I enjoyed it when the store was busy. Not only was it good for the bottom line but it made the time go by faster.

"So who's the guy?" Tara asked after the crowd cleared out.

"His name is Alex Turner and he's looking for a temp job. He goes to the university in Portland and wants to spend the holiday on the island. We'd just talked about looking for some temporary help, so I asked him to wait with Ebenezer. I figure the fact that the guy hooked up with him is a sign that we should at least talk to him."

Tara looked toward the cat lounge, where the young man was sitting on the sofa with Ebenezer on his lap. He appeared to be talking to the cat, and the cat appeared to be listening intently. How adorable was that?

"I can't believe that cat came all the way over here on his own," Tara marveled.

"It's not the first time," I reminded her.

"I wonder how he gets from Balthazar Pottage's private island to San Juan Island to catch the ferry."

"I suspect he stows away on the various boats that go out to the island to deliver supplies. So, about Alex?"

Tara shrugged. "We do need the help. Let's talk to him."

Tara and I joined Alex in the cat lounge. Ebenezer trotted over to the corner and lay down. Apparently, his reason for being there wasn't urgent. Of course it occurred to me that his purpose for coming to the store might have been to bring Alex into our lives and he'd completed his job. At this point it was too soon to tell, but it seemed Alex was both intelligent and friendly, and we really did need some part-time help.

After chatting with him and having him fill out an application, Tara asked Alex to come back the next day, after she'd had a chance to check his references. Alex thanked us for our time and agreed to return the following day. I knew Tara liked to check things out thoroughly, but I was pretty sure we'd found the help we needed.

Chapter 4

Monday December 14

The wind whipped around the islands, making the trip to Balthazar Pottage's private island less than pleasant. The ferry ride from Madrona Island to San Juan Island hadn't been all that bad, but the water taxi from San Juan Island out to Pottage's place was rough enough to give pause to even the most seasoned fisherman. At least the gate was open when Ebenezer and I arrived. I wasn't looking forward to having to squeeze through the small opening in the wall again, as I had the previous week. Although we'd hired Alex and he was working out fantastically, we'd had a near record day on Saturday, followed by a long day of church and family on Sunday. I was exhausted.

Pottage must have heard the boat that brought me to the island arrive because he seemed to be waiting for me just on the other side of the thick wooden door. He opened it, greeted the cat, and ushered me inside before I even had a chance to knock. As I had on my previous visit, I followed him down the dark, cold hallway to the sitting room, where a merry fire was warming the room.

"I was surprised when Ebenezer showed up at my store," I began.

"I told you, he comes and goes as he pleases. If he came to you, he must have had a reason."

I couldn't imagine what that reason could be; he'd done nothing but sleep the entire weekend, but perhaps he really had brought Alex to us, or maybe he just wanted to make certain I'd return to the island today.

Pottage handed me the book and then settled into his chair. It was obvious he'd invited me to his home to finish the book, not to engage in idle chitchat. I took off my coat and hung it over the back of the sofa, then settled into the second chair that faced the fire and began to read.

The Phantom slowly, gravely, silently, approached. When it came near him, Scrooge bent down upon his knee; for in the very air through which this Spirit moved it seemed to scatter gloom and mystery.

It was shrouded in a deep black garment, which concealed its head, its face, its form, and left nothing of it visible save one outstretched hand. But for this it would have been difficult to detach its figure from the night, and separate it from the darkness by which it was surrounded.

He felt that it was tall and stately when it came beside him, and that its mysterious presence filled him with a solemn dread. He knew no more, for the Spirit neither spoke nor moved.

``I am in the presence of the Ghost of Christmas Yet To Come?" said Scrooge.

The Spirit answered not, but pointed onward with its hand.

``You are about to show me shadows of the things that have not happened, but will happen in the time before us," Scrooge pursued. ``Is that so, Spirit?"

The upper portion of the garment was contracted for an instant in its folds, as if the Spirit had inclined its head.

That was the only answer he received.

I continued with the book until I got to the end.

"That's such a nice story," I commented as I set the book aside.

"I see you brought another book." Pottage looked hungrily at the book I'd carried with me.

"I did, but before we begin another book I think we need to talk."

"About what?" Pottage asked.

"About the Bayview Apartments. You promised to at least consider other options to evicting the tenants if I came back to finish the story," I reminded him.

"And I've done as I promised," Pottage assured me.

"And...?" I encouraged.

"And there's no other reasonable option. Now, start the second book."

I stood up and faced the man, hoping my height advantage over his sitting form would make a difference. "I can't believe you're unable to come up with *any* other alternative."

"You saw the estimate for fixing up the units. What would you suggest?"

"I don't know," I admitted. "I do know that, if your reputation is correct, you have more money than you'll ever be able to spend. Perhaps you can fix up the building and let the tenants stay out of the goodness of your heart."

"You're asking me to do this huge thing for the tenants of that building, yet what have any of them ever done for me? What has *anyone* ever done for me?"

I frowned. "How about if I continue to read to you? I can come back every Monday."

"I would enjoy that, but we're talking about more than a hundred thousand dollars," Pottage pointed out.

I guess the man had a point.

"Although, there *is* something else you can do for me that might be worth that amount of money."

I smiled. "What? I'll do anything."

"You can help me find out what became of my son."

I hesitated. Find his son? Was he kidding? He had a serious look on his face, so I had to assume he was serious in making his request.

"You want me to find your son?" I asked. "He's been missing for a very long time. How am I supposed to find him?"

"I have no idea, but Ebenezer seems to think you're the one to help us. In fact, he's quite insistent on it. Will you do it?"

I looked at the cat and hesitated. It did seem that we were linked in some way, and cats had helped me solve mysteries equally as impossible as this in the past. "If I help you figure out what happened to your son you'll let the tenants stay?"

"I'll do better than that. I'll fix up the building and deed it to the residents. Will you help me?"

"I'll try."

Balthazar Pottage smiled.

"Do you have any idea where I should start?" I asked.

He stood up. "Come with me."

The man led me to a room toward the end of the hall that looked to be used for storage. He walked over to a box and instructed me to bring it back to the sitting room. I set the box on the table and Pottage took off the top.

"Contained in this box is everything I've collected over the years in my attempt to find my son. There are newspaper articles, photos, police reports, and a list of everyone who was at the party on the day Charles disappeared."

"Okay. Why don't you tell me exactly what happened that day?"

Pottage returned to his chair and settled in, so I went back to the chair I'd been sitting in as well. I had a feeling I was in for a long and not at all pleasant story.

"It was Christmas Eve. Charles was six weeks old and we'd decided to have him baptized. After the ceremony we held a reception. Belle put Charles in the crib in his room, which was located upstairs in the nursery, next to the master suite. Later that afternoon Belle went up to check on him and found the crib empty."

"So someone who was at the reception must have taken him," I concluded.

"Perhaps, but the christening was heavily guarded. I made my money by cashing in on the misfortunes of others. I had a lot of enemies. Entrance to the gated estate could only be accessed by those who had an invitation. I had a security guard at the gate to ensure against those who might attempt to crash the party. There wasn't a single person present who I could imagine would have wanted to harm Charles."

"Someone took him," I insisted.

"Yes, someone did."

I sat back as I considered the situation. On one hand, a limited suspect pool was going to make the investigation easier. On the other, the fact that all the suspects appeared on the surface to be family and friends of the couple was going to make things more complicated. I realized I would need to carefully comb through the facts to determine a possible motive where none was immediately apparent.

"It seems to me," I began, "that one of your guests must have snuck upstairs during the reception, taken the baby, and then snuck back out of the house."

"Perhaps. Although we had a guard posted at the top of the stairs. His orders were not to allow access to the second story to anyone other than Belle, myself, and the nanny. I don't see how the kidnapper could have reached the nursery without first getting past the guard."

"Maybe the nanny was the kidnapper," I suggested.

"She never left the second floor. The guard verified that. They found her sleeping on the lounge in the little room just off Charles's nursery. She swore she never saw anyone come upstairs other than Belle to check on the baby."

It figures this would be a complicated mystery. Of course, if it hadn't been complicated, it would have been solved years ago. I looked at the guest list. On the surface it didn't seem likely that anyone at the party would kidnap the child, but I didn't have anything to lose by looking into the kidnapping further. If nothing else it might buy me some time to figure out another solution for the occupants of the apartments.

"Okay, I'll see what I can do. In the meantime, will you rescind the eviction notices? I'll need some time to figure this out."

"I'll tell my attorney to put a hold on the evictions until after the first of the year. I imagine that will give you enough time?"

"Less than a month to solve a decades' old mystery the cops couldn't solve at the time? Piece of cake," I said sarcastically.

"Good. Then it appears we have a deal. Perhaps you should take Ebenezer with you. I do worry about him traveling on the ferry by himself. You can return him after you've found my son."

"Are you sure you want to take this on?" Cody asked later that evening as we sat at my kitchen table and sorted through the contents of the box, which Balthazar Pottage had insisted I take with me. It was still snowing outside and holiday music serenaded us. It should have been a romantic evening, but instead we were discussing a kidnapping that would probably be impossible to solve.

"I have to," I said. "Pottage has agreed to postpone the evictions while I work on this, so at the very least the tenants will get a brief reprieve. And if I can solve the mystery, he's promised not only to fix up the building but to sign the units over to the people who are living in them."

"Did he sign a contract to that effect?"

"No, but I heard him call and speak to his attorney about postponing the evictions. I mean really, what do I have to lose? If I try to figure this out and am not successful, I'm out a little time, but the tenants will still have had the benefit of the delay in the eviction process. If I succeed they'll have homes no one can ever take away from them."

Cody shrugged. "I'm in. Where do we start?"

"I'm not sure. There's a lot of information here. Maybe we should call the gang."

I called Tara, Danny, Finn, and Siobhan and asked them if they could meet me at the cabin for dinner. Finn was the resident deputy for Madrona Island and Siobhan was my older sister and Finn's girlfriend. They'd all helped me solve mysteries in the past and I hoped they could help with this one as well. They confirmed that they were free and would love to come for dinner. I whipped together a quick casserole while Cody made a salad and buttered a loaf of sourdough bread. Cody and I worked well together and it filled me with contentment as we prepared the meal for our friends.

Christmas jazz played in the background and the scent of the bayberry candles I'd bought from the bookstore filled the air. The ocean just beyond my cabin was angrier than usual, making a crashing sound that could be heard even over the music, but I chose to enjoy the steady rhythm rather than be annoyed by it.

Once everyone had arrived, we ate before we gathered in the living room in front of the fireplace and began to discuss strategy.

"How are we supposed to solve a kidnapping that happened twenty years ago?" Danny asked as he nibbled on one of the brownies I'd made for dessert.

"I'm not sure," I admitted. "What I do know is that the crime occurred on *this* island. Someone must know something. Besides, Pottage has actually managed to accumulate quite a bit of information over the years. I'm kind of surprised he hasn't already figured the whole thing out."

"If he's been working on it for twenty years and hasn't figured it out what makes him think you'll be able to?" Tara asked.

"Ebenezer told him that I was the key to finding the answer."

"The cat?" Finn asked.

"Hey, stranger things have happened. Besides, what do we have to lose? If we figure this out Cody will have a fantastic story for the newspaper and we'll all have the satisfaction of knowing we helped twelve families find a permanent home."

"I'm in," Siobhan assured me. "The whole thing has grabbed my interest. I say we start with everyone who was in the house on the night of the kidnapping. Someone must have seen something. We'll need a mystery board."

"I'll go get Maggie's whiteboard," Danny offered.

Cody and I quickly did the dishes while Danny went up to the main house. The use of a mystery board while we worked through the details had been Siobhan's suggestion when we were trying to solve a confusing series of murders in October, and it had ended up making all the difference. If there was one thing you could say about Siobhan, she was organized, and she knew how to take charge of a project. Since she'd returned to the island she'd been serving as temporary mayor and doing a fantastic job.

When Danny returned with the board we listed everyone who was on the Pottage property the day of the kidnapping. I went through the list the old man had given me while Siobhan used a dry erase marker to transfer the list to the whiteboard.

She began by listing Father Kilian, who had performed the christening. I volunteered to speak to him the next day because it would be easy to stop by the church on my lunch break to see what he could remember from the day.

Belle's sister, Bonnie, and Bonnie's husband, Sutton, were also in attendance. They were listed as the godparents. Belle's cousin, Jessica, and her husband, Brad, were there, as well as Belle's best friend, Beverly, and Beverly's husband, Steve.

According to Pottage's notes, Bonnie and Sutton, Jessica and Brad, and Beverly and Steve all lived out of state and were staying at the residence when the kidnapping occurred. They remained at the house for a couple of days after Charles was taken, and they all helped out with the search effort. I doubted any of them would have kidnapped Charles, and it wasn't going to be easy to interview them, but I had Siobhan list them anyway.

Mayor Bradley and his wife, Nora, had attended the party, as had Doris Rutherford and her husband, Ted. Both Mayor Bradley and Ted Rutherford had since passed away, but it would be worth my time, I was certain, to chat with both Doris and Nora.

My neighbor Francine Rivers had been invited, as had the previous owner of the *Madrona Island News*, Orson Cobalter. Orson most likely was there to cover the event for the paper, but I couldn't imagine why Francine had been in attendance. Orson had since passed and so was unavailable for questioning, but it would be easy to pop next door to talk with Francine, which I offered to do.

Surprisingly, my Aunt Maggie was on the guest list, as was her best friend and business partner Marley Donnelly. I figured a conversation with the two women would be a good place to start. They worked just a few doors down from Coffee Cat Books, so a quick trip down the street during a slow time of the day should net the results we required.

There were five other names mentioned. Edith Cribbage had been the nanny, Jane Partridge the maid, Liza Bolton the cook, Roger Riverton the upstairs guard, and Phillip Preston the guard at the gate. It had been a very long time and I didn't know any of them, but I hoped I could track them down at some point during the investigation. My gut told mc it was an employee and not a guest who would turn out to be the kidnapper.

"On the surface, do any of these people seem to have a motive to kidnap the baby?" Siobhan asked.

"I don't know the out-of-town guests, but it seems unlikely any of them is guilty of the crime," I answered. "For one thing, they remained at the estate for a couple of days following the kidnapping. If one of them was guilty they would have had to find a place to stash the baby until they left. That seems unlikely. As for the local guests, there's not a single person I would believe guilty of such a crime."

"Yet someone did it," Danny pointed out.

"Yes," I agreed, "someone did. I plan to speak to everyone on the list, but right now my money is on one of the staff as the guilty party. The problem is I have absolutely no idea where to find any of them. I guess I'll start with the people on the list who I know to see if anyone can point me in a direction."

Chapter 5

Tuesday, December 15

"Both the peppermint lattes and the chocolate mochas are on sale this week," I informed the group of teens who had come into the bookstore for a hot beverage after school.

"Two of each," a tall girl with long blond hair replied. "Do you think you'll have the gingerbread latte on sale again?"

"We had the gingerbread last week, but I think Tara plans to feature it again," I answered. "Do you all have plans for break?" I asked as I prepared the drinks.

"I'm going to Aspen," the blonde informed me.

"That sounds like fun." I set her drink in front of her.

"It would have been if my boyfriend could have come, but my parents are torturing us with a family-only trip. I mean, really, who sets out to torture their kid at Christmas?"

"At least you get to go skiing," one of the other girls, a brunette, added. "I have to stay home and babysit my two little brothers while Mom's at work."

"That's such a drag," the blonde agreed.

"That will be twelve dollars," I informed the group after I had delivered all the drinks. "Be sure to check back next week. I'll see what I can do about the gingerbread."

"Who's the cute guy reading to that bunch of kids?" one of the teens asked.

"Yeah, he'll do," another of the girls joined in. "Is he single?"

"His name is Alex. I don't know if he's single, but I can tell you he'll be working here over Christmas break."

"He's a total babe. Does he live on the island?" the first girl asked.

"Afraid not. Besides, he's too old for you. He goes to the university in Portland."

"Such a shame," the blonde sighed. "I wouldn't mind finding him under my tree on Christmas morning."

I smiled at the girls, who were almost tripping over their own feet as they stared at Alex as they walked away. He really was good-looking, but not as good-looking as my Cody. Still, I was sure he did quite well in the girlfriend department.

I smiled in greeting at the next customer. "What can I get for you?"

"We're here about a cat," the woman, who I didn't recognize, informed me.

"Awesome. Let me get Tara to cover the counter and we can go next door to chat."

I ushered the woman and her daughter toward the cat lounge as soon as I informed Tara what I was doing.

"So, what sort of a cat are you looking for?" I asked.

"A kitten," the girl answered.

"Susie saw a black and white kitten in here on Saturday. She's been bugging me to come to take a look at it ever since. I don't see it today. Have you sold it?"

"First of all, we don't sell the cats and kittens we feature here. We adopt them out to prescreened families. And yes, I do still have the black and white kitten. It's at the cat sanctuary today. I try to rotate the cats I bring into the lounge. I can give you an application to fill out, but I want to be sure you really want a kitten and are willing and able to take care of it. I don't mean to be rude, but adopting a pet because you want your daughter to stop pestering you isn't a good reason."

The woman frowned at me. I had the sense she wasn't at all sold on the idea of actually caring for a kitten.

"Please, Mom? You promised me a treat if I was good during this boring business trip. We've been here for five days and I've been good. I want a kitten," the little girl insisted.

"If I get the kitten for you will you shut up about it?"

The irritated look on the woman's face pretty much made up my mind that I wasn't going to hand over one of my cats to this particular family.

"Like I said, we have an adoption process. I really can't promise you anything until we do a background check," I informed the woman.

"You do a background check on people who simply want to adopt a kitten?" the woman asked.

"Yes, we do."

"Thanks, but no thanks. The whole thing sounds like a hassle."

"But Mom..." the girl whined as the woman turned to leave.

"I'm really too busy for all this," the woman said to the child. "I still need to meet with the old geezer out on the island. We'll go to the pet store in Seattle next weekend, where they don't give you the third degree to buy a kitten."

"Old geezer," I interrupted. "Do you mean Balthazar Pottage?"

"Yes. I work for the development company that plans to build condos on his land. I'm stuck on this island until I can convince him to follow through with his initial promise to sell the land to my boss. Trust me, there's nothing I want more than to be on the next ferry heading east. But the only way I can do that is if I can talk some sense into the old guy. Wish me luck."

Hardly.

The woman's words left me with a nervous feeling. Not that I actually thought Pottage would back out of our deal. He really did seem to want to find out what had happened to his son. Still, the knowledge that the condo developer was putting pressure on him did fill me with a certain level of urgency.

I checked on all the cats and then returned to the coffee bar.

"It looks like we're through the morning rush. Would you mind if I take both an early and a long lunch so I can go talk to a couple of the people from the list we made last night?" I asked Tara.

"Go ahead," Tara said. "Alex and I should be fine until people start gathering for the three o'clock ferry."

"Thanks. I'll hurry."

I decided my first stop would be the Bait and Stitch. Both Maggie and Marley should be there at this time of day, and chances were good that Doris Rutherford would be there as well. It was a nice day, so I decided to walk the short distance between the stores. I wasn't sure what information, if any, the women could provide, but I was enjoying my walk.

Madrona Island was a magical place during the holidays. Everyone went out of their way to provide a welcoming feel. White twinkle lights were strung in the trees along Main before Halloween and continued to light the otherwise dark street until after the short days of winter gave way to the longer ones of spring. The shops along Main had gone all out with their decorations. Windows featured holiday scenes and almost every door featured a bright green wreath. Holiday music could be heard from each shop as I passed.

As with the other businesses, the soft sounds of Christmas CDs playing holiday tunes greeted me as I opened the door to the Bait and Stitch. The shop my aunt and Marley owned was a unique endeavor, a warm and friendly store that combined Maggie's love of fishing with Marley's love of sewing. It also served as gossip central because the women of Madrona Island tended to congregate around the quilting tables to share news, real or imagined, while enjoying cups of tea.

"Cait, how nice to see you." Marley hugged me as I walked in through the front door.

"The place looks great. I especially love the red bows you've placed around the sales floor. Very festive."

"Maggie and I had the best time decorating," Marley said.

"Coffee Cat Books looks lovely as well," Doris Rutherford, the queen bee of the local gossip hotline, commented from one of the chairs Marley had placed around the quilting table.

"Yes, you girls have done a nice job with the place," added Ruth Everson, the local charity events coordinator.

"Thank you both. Tara and I worked really hard to bring the feeling of the season to the store. Is Maggie around?"

"She's over on the fishing supplies side of the building with a customer," Marley informed me. "I'm sure she'll come back here after she's finished. Things are pretty slow on the fishing end of things at this time of year."

"Cait, I heard you're the person responsible for saving the Bayview Apartments," Ruth commented. "My aunt lives in the building and she told me how you took charge to save the day."

"Yeah, well, it isn't a sure thing yet. I'm trying my best to save the building, but I'm afraid it really is a bit of a long shot."

"How can we help?" Marley asked.

"Yes, what can we do?" Ruth seconded.

"Perhaps a committee to address the issue," Doris suggested.

"A committee to address what issue?" Maggie asked as she walked into the sewing room.

"The issue of the Bayview Apartments," I informed Maggie. "I've worked out a deal of sorts with Balthazar Pottage, but in order to save the building in the long run I need to figure out what happened to his son."

Maggie frowned. "That's not going to be an easy task."

"Tell me about it. I understand you were at the party the day of Charles Pottage's disappearance."

"I was," Maggie confirmed. "As were Marley and Doris. We shared everything we could possibly remember with the deputies who investigated the case at the time. Nothing we told them seemed to help then and I really doubt it will now."

"Maybe not, but I have to try."

"Certainly. Have a seat," Marley offered.

"What would you like to know?" Doris asked.

"I was curious as to why the three of you were even at the christening party," I began.

"When she first moved to the island, Belle Pottage joined the local garden club, of which the three of us were members," Maggie informed me. "She wasn't much of a gardener; I think it was a way for her to meet people. Her husband wasn't around all that much, and she was pretty much stuck in that big house by herself most of the time. We felt sorry for her and went out of our way to befriend her."

"What exactly happened on the day of the kidnapping?" I asked.

"The party was for the christening of Charles Pottage," Maggie began.

"He really was a beautiful baby," Marley added.

"And he had all that thick dark hair," Doris joined in.

"Father Kilian performed the ceremony," Maggie said. "Belle's sister and brother-in-law were present to act as godparents."

"And after the christening?" I wondered.

"Belle took Charles upstairs for a nap. He'd been fussy throughout the ceremony."

"What did everyone else do while Belle was upstairs with the baby?"

"The Pottages put on quite a spread. I'm pretty sure everyone stayed to eat. Father Kilian left shortly after the ceremony because he had Mass to perform, but everyone else mingled while we enjoyed the delicious food and wine."

I pulled the list Pottage had given me out of my pocket and considered the names. "It appears it was actually a fairly small party."

"It was," Maggie agreed. "Keep in mind, Balthazar Pottage hadn't made any friends on the island and Belle had only made a few. It was Christmas Eve and most people were home with their families. Marley and I weren't due to share Christmas with your family until the next day, so we decided to attend the gathering, more as a show of support for Belle than anything else."

"And Ted and I didn't have family on the island, so we welcomed the diversion," Doris offered.

"Do you remember who else from the island was there?"

Maggie paused as she appeared to be considering my question. "Mayor Bradley was there with Nora. The Bradleys didn't stay all that long after the actual christening. I'm sure they'd left before Belle discovered Charles was missing."

"Belle had also invited a cousin and a couple of friends from out of state," Marley added. "I believe all the out-of-town guests were staying at the house."

"Does it seem odd to you that Belle chose Christmas Eve as the date for her baby's christening?" I asked the women.

"I don't think Belle was happy in her marriage," Maggie offered. "If I had to guess I'd say she held the christening then as an excuse to invite her sister and friends to stay on the island for the holiday."

I frowned. "How unhappy was she?"

Maggie shrugged. "It's hard to know what's in another's heart, and she didn't really speak of her relationship with her much older husband, but he was away a lot of the time and she commented several times that she preferred it that way. I think she hoped the baby would change things, but if you ask me I think Charles just drove a larger wedge between the couple. If Charles hadn't been kidnapped and Belle hadn't been killed in the car accident, my prediction is the marriage wouldn't have lasted."

I looked down at my list again. "Mr. Pottage told me that there were two guards on site that day, one at the gate and one at the top of the stairs. Doesn't that seem excessive considering the only guests were family and friends?"

"I thought so at the time." Doris nodded. "But I learned later that he had received death threats after he evicted a bunch of people from an apartment building he'd purchased out of bankruptcy. I think the guard at the gate was always there, but I'm not certain why he added the one at the top of the stairs. It did seem a bit much."

Maggie looked up as the bell over the door rang. Two couples I didn't know walked in from the cold. Maggie got up to chat with them, effectively ending the conversation, but I felt like I had a bit more insight into the day's events.

"Do any of you know where I can find Edith Cribbage, Jane Partridge, Liza Bolton, Phillip Preston, or Roger Riverton?" I asked the women who were left at the table.

"Jane works over at the Cove," Doris supplied, mentioning a lodging property on the east shore.

"And Phillip Preston is the man who owns that guns and ammo shop in Harthaven," Ruth added.

"Thanks to all of you for taking the time to share your memories."

"Any time, dear." Marley patted my hand. "I just wish we could have been of more help."

I knew exactly where the guns and ammo store was, even though I'd never been inside it, and I figured it wouldn't take long for me to have a chat with the man, so I decided to approach Phillip Preston next. If everyone who both arrived and left the house had to drive past him, he must have some insight as to who was still inside at the time Charles's disappearance was discovered.

Chapter 6

Like Pelican Bay, the village of Harthaven was decorated for the upcoming holiday. Although I enjoy living on the peninsula and working in Pelican Bay, Harthaven was the place that most felt like home. I was born and raised in the predominantly Catholic blue-collar fishing village. I attended Harthaven Elementary School and Madrona Island High School and I'd spent almost every Sunday of my life worshipping with my family at St. Patrick's. In some ways I felt Pelican Bay represented my future, while Harthaven held my past and the roots of my family.

Phillip Preston was there when I arrived at the guns and ammo shop, as Ruth had indicated he probably would be. He confirmed that both Mayor Bradley and his wife and Father Kilian had left the Pottage estate before the discovery that Charles was missing. He also assured me that no other guests arrived or departed during the time period between when Charles was taken upstairs and the discovery of the kidnapping. I doubted either Father Kilian or the mayor had kidnapped the child, so had the kidnapper gotten away?

Preston also confirmed that Pottage was concerned for his family's safety because he had received threatening letters, after which he'd hired several security guards to man the gate 24/7. Preston just happened to be the guard on duty at the time of the kidnapping. The only other item of interest Preston offered was that after the threats began coming in, neither Belle nor Charles left the estate for any reason, and poor Mrs. Pottage hadn't been permitted any company after Charles was born with the exception of the staff, who came and went on a daily basis, and the guests who arrived for the christening.

I still had a little time before I had to get back to the bookstore, so after I left Preston, I headed over to the church to speak with Father Kilian. I doubted he could add much that I hadn't already verified, and he'd left before the kidnapping occurred, but he was an intelligent man with a keen eye, so it couldn't hurt to have a chat with him.

I explained to Father Kilian why I was there and he escorted me into his office and closed the door behind us. He offered me a glass of water before he began.

"I remember the day of the baptism well," he began. "Normally we hold christenings in the church, but Mrs. Pottage insisted that her husband would never allow a ceremony there and she really wanted to have the baby baptized, so I agreed to go to their home. When I arrived I could sense the tension between Mr. and Mrs. Pottage. I wasn't able to speak to them alone because there were others around, but the fact that they were clearly not getting along was evident to everyone."

"Did you see anything at all that might offer a clue as to what could have happened to Baby Charles?" I asked. "Someone who didn't belong? An extra vehicle? One of the guests acting out of character?"

"You're probably the tenth person who has asked me those same questions in the past twenty years, but no, not really. I arrived early to set up for the ceremony and left shortly after it was over to prepare for Mass. It was a pity to have to leave. I managed to get a look at the buffet table and it looked as if the caterer had done a fantastic job."

"The party was catered?" Father Kilian was the first person to mention caterers.

"Yes, and quite lavishly."

"Do you remember the name of the catering company?"

"The caterer was a woman, but I don't recall her name. She didn't stay long after she delivered the food. The Pottage cook was on the premises that day. I understand, based on what others have said, that it was the cook who served the food and then stayed to clean up."

"Why didn't they just have the cook prepare the food?"

"I'm afraid I don't know. I didn't speak to the cook and I only spoke to the caterer for a moment. I noticed her packing her van to leave when I walked out to my car after the christening, so I stopped to compliment her on the beautiful spread."

"Do you know how long that was after Mrs. Pottage took the baby upstairs?"

"Not long. Maybe fifteen or twenty minutes."

I looked at the clock. I really needed to go if I hoped to be back at the bookstore in time to help Tara with the three o'clock ferry passengers.

"Well, thank you for taking the time to share what you remembered with me. If you think of anything else please let me know."

"I will. I hope you find the answer Mr. Pottage is seeking. It can't have been easy to live with such uncertainty for so many years."

"It's a good thing you thought to borrow Danny's truck," I said to Cody later that evening as we loaded the six Christmas trees we'd just purchased into the bed of the vehicle.

It had been Mr. Parsons's request that had led to the picking up of the trees. He wasn't able to get around all that well and had asked Cody, who lived with him, if he would be willing to fetch him a tree. Cody had promised to pick one up for him that evening; he'd been thinking about getting one for his third-floor apartment anyway.

Cody had called to ask me to come along with him, and because I didn't have a tree yet, we decided we'd just pick up all three. Then my mom called while I was waiting for Cody to pick me up, and when I mentioned where I was going, she'd asked if I could pick up a tree for her as well. That brought us up to four.

The fifth tree came into play when Cody went downstairs to tell Mr. Parsons he was leaving. Francine Rivers was visiting and asked if he could pick one up for her too. We were just pulling away from my cabin when my Aunt Maggie came by and asked if we could get a tree for her as long as we were at it.

"I feel like Santa loading up to make his deliveries." Cody grinned as he tied a rope around the full load to prevent it from shifting during the drive.

"You make an adorable Santa." I smiled as I pulled on the end of Cody's red and white Santa hat before leaning in for a quick kiss.

"What do you say we deliver these trees, pick up a pizza, and then decorate yours?" Cody suggested. "I'm feeling downright festive tonight."

"Sounds good to me." I opened the door for Max to jump on to the bench seat before me. "The secret to the success of our plan is to somehow prevent my mother from roping us into a long conversation when we deliver her tree. She seems more amped up than usual about the holiday this year. Every time I see her she asks about the various family events she has planned for the holiday weekend."

"I'm quite enjoying your mother's enthusiasm," Cody commented. "It's been a long time since I've had the opportunity to enjoy a good old-fashioned family Christmas."

"Yeah, I guess Christmas must not be quite the same when you're stationed overseas."

"Not at all," Cody confirmed.

"I'm looking forward to spending Christmas with my family, but it will be nice to spend a quiet Christmas Eve together. Just the two of us."

"Yeah, about that...I wanted to talk to you about our plans."

"Our plans?"

"I know we discussed spending the evening alone together, but because I'll be at your mother's with you on Christmas Day, I thought maybe we could make dinner for Mr. Parsons on Christmas Eve. He doesn't have anyone else and I hate to think of him not having a Christmas."

"That's a wonderful idea." I smiled. "Maybe we should invite Francine and Banjo and Summer as well. It will feel more like a celebration with a houseful of people."

Cody leaned over and kissed me. "That's why I love you. You're always willing to think of the happiness of others."

"Hey, it was your idea. It'll be fun."

"It will. Let's deliver your mom's tree first and then we'll drop off Francine's. We can ask her about Christmas Eve while we're there."

"Sounds like a plan. Besides, I've been wanting to talk to Francine about Charles Pottage's christening. I'll ask her a few questions while you set her tree in the stand for her."

"How's the investigation going?" Cody asked as he pulled out of the tree lot and into traffic.

"Slowly. I'm not sure I'm going to be able to solve this one. I've spoken to about half of the people on Pottage's list and no one seems to have seen anything. It appears as if Baby Charles simply disappeared."

"Have you spoken to the nanny?" Cody asked as he turned off the main street and headed toward the highway that would take us to my mother's house. "She was the only one, other than the guard at the top of the stairs, who was upstairs the entire time. It seems reasonable that she would have seen or heard something."

"No, not yet," I answered. "I'm hoping to track them both down in the next day or two. Juggling the investigation with my job at the bookstore and the upcoming holiday is proving to be a bit of a challenge. By the way, did you ever find out if the costumes for the play are going to be finished on time?"

"I called and spoke to the woman who agreed to make them. She promised me that we'll have them in time for the dress rehearsal."

"Good. I was worried we'd have to throw together makeshift costumes at the last minute."

Our conversation paused as we pulled up in front of the house where my mother lived with my younger sister Cassie and my older brother Aiden, when he wasn't away fishing. Luckily, Aiden was home and available to help Cody carry the fifteen-foot tree into the living room, where the tree stand was set up and waiting. Mom insisted that Cody and I stay for a cup of hot cocoa, but happily she didn't launch into a long discussion that would require us to stay for longer than it took to drink our beverage and eat one of the cookies she'd baked that day.

Next on our list was Francine Rivers. Cody unloaded her six-foot tree while I followed her into the kitchen, where she'd headed to make coffee.

"I really appreciate you and Cody bringing the tree for me. I wasn't sure I was even going to get one this year. The man who used to deliver mine closed his lot and moved off the island and there was no way I could fetch a tree in my little car."

"We were happy to do it," I assured her.

"Would you like a cookie? I just made them today."

"Thank you," I said, politely taking one. "As long as I'm here, I was wondering if I could ask you a few questions about Charles Pottage's christening."

"Mr. Parsons mentioned you were investigating his kidnapping when I was at his place earlier today.

I'm not sure I know anything that will help you, but ask away."

I set my half-eaten cookie down on the Santa napkin Francine had provided.

"I'm curious why you were at the baptism in the first place."

"I met Belle Pottage when she joined the garden club I belonged to with your Aunt Maggie and a few others. Maggie was invited to the christening as well."

"Yes, I spoke to her about it, but I didn't realize you were a member of the same club. What can you remember about Belle?"

"She was a nice woman who seemed a little lonely. Her much older and very busy husband moved her to the island shortly after they married. His business was based in Seattle and I don't think he visited his bride all that often. Belle hadn't made a lot of friends, but she seemed to really appreciate those she had. After she became pregnant her participation in the garden club lessened considerably, but there were a few of us—myself and Maggie and a couple of others—who stayed in touch with her."

"I heard that once Balthazar Pottage began getting threatening letters he basically limited her movements to the estate."

"Yes, that's true. I felt bad for her. She seemed very unhappy. It appeared that she adored her baby, but I had the feeling she regretted marrying such a forceful and controlling man. In many ways he treated her more like a child than a wife."

I took a sip of the coffee Francine had set in front of me before continuing.

"Did you notice anything at all odd on the day of the christening that might lead to a clue as to what happened to Baby Charles?"

Francine paused, I assumed to consider my question. "No. It was the oddest thing. There really is no logical explanation as to how the baby could have turned up missing. We were all downstairs during the ceremony. When the baptism was over Belle took Charles upstairs to feed him and put him down for a nap. The only person up there at the time was the nanny, who, based on what I've heard, was napping herself in the little room just off the nursery. There was a guard at the top of the stairs to ensure that no one who wasn't authorized to do so accessed the second story of the house. There's simply no way anyone could have taken that baby, but apparently someone did, and right under the nose of a houseful of people."

"Do you know if there's a back staircase?"

Francine thought about it. "Not that I know of, but I didn't search the entire house, so maybe. I guess that would be a good question for Balthazar Pottage."

"Did you notice anyone acting oddly during the christening?"

"No, not really. Once it was over and Belle took Charles upstairs everyone else helped themselves to the delicious buffet lunch. After she'd gotten the baby to sleep Belle joined us and actually seemed to be in an exceptionally good mood."

"And Pottage?" I asked. "What was he doing during the luncheon?"

Francine frowned. "I don't recall. I imagine he was mingling with the guests, but I didn't speak to him myself. I'm sure he must have been there, though."

"So Belle came downstairs after putting the baby down for a nap. When exactly did she notice he was missing?" I asked.

"It must have been about an hour later. Maybe more. Everyone was finished eating and most of us were saying our good-byes, although there were still several people at the bar that had been set up. I believe some of the guests were actually staying at the house. Anyway, Belle went back upstairs to check on Charles and the next thing we knew, she was standing at the top of the stairs screaming that he wasn't there. Tripp Brimmer was called in and a thorough investigation of the house was conducted, but the baby had simply vanished."

Tripp was the resident deputy for Madrona Island at the time of the kidnapping.

"Everyone was questioned, but no one admitted to having seen anything," Francine went on. "It was simply horrifying. I felt so awful for Belle. She was hysterical, as one can imagine."

"Yes, I can."

Cody walked into the kitchen. "The tree's in the stand and ready to be decorated. Do you need me to bring out your decorations?"

"Would you, dear? They're in the basement in green tubs with red tops."

"No problem," Cody said and headed downstairs.

"That's quite a nice young man you've got yourself there." Francine beamed.

"Yeah, he's the best."

"It warms my heart the way he looks after Mr. Parsons. He goes out of his way to make sure he eats right and has plenty of company. I know Mr. Parsons appreciates everything he does for him more than he can say."

"Cody really cares about Mr. Parsons. He thinks of him as an honorary grandfather. And I know he enjoys his apartment on the third floor of the house. It provides him with some privacy while also allowing him to feel like part of a family."

I could hear Cody moving things around in the space below the kitchen.

"Cody and I plan to make dinner for Mr. Parsons on Christmas Eve," I added. "We'd like you to come if you aren't busy."

"Why, I'd love to. It does get lonely at times over the holidays. Do you mind if I bring Nora Bradley along? It's her first Christmas since the mayor passed. I know the couple was in the process of divorcing, but Nora is still taking his death pretty hard. I'd planned to suggest to her that we do something together because, like me, she has no other family to spend the holiday with."

"We'd be happy to have Nora," I said. "We plan to ask Banjo and Summer as well, so we'll have a nice little group."

"I'm really looking forward to it."

I accepted a second cookie from Francine and added delicately, "Before we go I wanted to ask about Belle's accident."

"It was such a tragedy," Francine murmured. "The first few days after Charles went missing were complete and total chaos as the whole island was searched. I believe her visitors left after a few days and Belle was left in the house with only her husband, who was even more distraught, it seemed, than she was. She must have felt she needed some distance, because I heard she left the house during a storm. Her car slid off the road and she was killed."

"Do you know where she was going?" I asked.

"I didn't speak to her after the party, but I heard she was heading to the harbor. There was a newspaper report that she'd hired a boat to take her to the mainland, where she was going to meet a friend."

"She was taking a boat in the middle of a storm?" I asked.

"Yes, that does seem odd. I guess I never really stopped to think about it before."

Cody came back into the room. "I'm all set. The boxes are next to the tree."

"Thank you. I do appreciate it."

I got up from the bar stool I was sitting on. "Thanks for the input. Francine. Let me know if anything else comes to mind."

"I'll do that. You know, perhaps you should speak to the best friend. I believe her name was Beverly. Maybe she would know what Belle was really doing on the road during one of the stormiest days the island had seen for quite some time."

Chapter 7

Thursday, December 17

I pulled the covers up over my head against the chill in my room. At some point during the night the fire had died. I'd been exhausted by the time I'd gotten home from play rehearsal that night and hadn't renewed the wood stove the way I should have.

Ebenezer, who was burrowed under the covers with me, swatted at my nose as Max, who most likely needed to go out, began to move around the room. I slowly lowered the heavy comforter to peek out. It was snowing again, and if the ice on the windows was any indication, it appeared it was going to be a blustery day.

"Fifteen more minutes," I groaned as the animals began to grow impatient at my unwillingness to get up despite the fact that I was already most likely going to be late for work.

Max pulled at the covers, which caused me to quite reluctantly roll out of bed. I pulled on my heaviest sweatshirt and knee-high slippers and shivered my way downstairs. I let Max out through the side door, then restarted the fire in both the wood stove and the small fireplace in the living room. Then I started a pot of coffee and fed Ebenezer while it brewed.

Although I was freezing, the sight that greeted me through the windows was magical. Large snowflakes drifted through the air before falling into the ocean, which was nicely calm this morning.

Max barked to let me know he wanted back in. I dried his coat and fed him before pouring my first cup of coffee. I took it into the living room, where I curled up in front of the fire with one of the quilts Maggie had made for me.

The tree Cody and I had decorated on Tuesday evening lent a holiday feel to the room. I used the remote to turn on the lights so I could enjoy them while I sipped my morning brew. I wasn't certain what to get for Cody for Christmas. I wanted something a bit more meaningful and personal than a sweater or a wallet, but I wasn't sure we were in the place in our relationship where sexy underwear or silk pajamas were appropriate either.

Of course we'd been sharing an intimate relationship for over a month, and something black and silky would look oh so good on his hard, fit frame.

I leaned my head back against the sofa to further engage in my daydream about Cody and the imaginary gift I was sure I'd never have the courage to get for him when I heard a crash. I opened my eyes and looked around the room. Ebenezer had knocked my backpack off the table and the contents had spilled out on the floor. One of the items that had been in the bag I carried with me everywhere was an envelope filled with some of the newspaper articles, the police report, and various photographs of Charles that had been in the box Balthazar Pottage had given me. Apparently Ebenezer wanted me to work on the case while I sipped my coffee rather than daydreaming about Cody in black silk boxers.

I reluctantly got up, refilled my cup, and picked up the stuff on the floor. I brought the envelope over to the sofa and slipped out the contents. The first document was the initial report written by Tripp Brimmer. I hadn't gotten around to speaking to Tripp yet; perhaps today.

The report detailed pretty much everything I'd already learned, and it clarified that access to the second story, where the nursery was located, had been limited to the main staircase, which had been guarded the entire evening.

I thought about that some more.

First of all, the fact that there was a guard on duty was odd. I understood Pottage was concerned about the safety of his family, but there was a guard at the gate monitoring access to the estate and everyone in the house that day were family or friends. Did Pottage anticipate a particular threat to his baby? And if so, from whom? I wished I had the old man's phone number so I could call him; there was no way I'd have time to visit with him before Monday.

The other thing I couldn't help but consider was whether the upstairs guard was in on the abduction. If the only access to and from the second story was past that man, and the baby was somehow removed from that floor, it made sense that he must have been working with the kidnapper. The first thing on my list today, after I checked in with Tara, was going to be to track down and interview Roger Riverton. Maybe he could shed some light on what had really happened that day.

I got up once again to retrieve the small notepad I kept in my backpack. I wrote down: *interview Tripp Brimmer and Roger Riverton* as tasks one and two for the day, then added *pick up milk* and *ask Danny about a Christmas gift for Aiden*. Aiden was a tough one to buy for, but Danny usually had an idea or two.

I clicked my pen open and closed as I considered the report in my hand. Charles had been kidnapped on December 24. Belle's out-of-town guests had left the island on December 27 and she was killed in an auto accident on December 29, just five days after her baby was kidnapped. Five days seemed much too soon to give up completely and leave the island to my mind. Could it be that there was another reason she was driving her car on icy roads in the middle of a storm? The only account of why she had been on the road was that provided by her husband. I supposed he was the logical person to ask, but the whole thing didn't seem quite right.

After I finished my coffee I took a quick shower and dressed in warm clothes, then gathered the cats I planned to feature in the cat lounge that day and headed into town. The snow was little more than flurries and unlikely to amount to any accumulation, but the chill in the air was enough to make me want to go home and crawl back into my bed.

Unfortunately, returning to the warmth of my little cabin wasn't in the cards. After settling the cats in the lounge, I helped Tara and Alex with the traffic from the first ferry of the day and then headed back out to see if I could track down Tripp and/or Finn. The two resident deputies, one retired and one active, seemed like the best place to start the day's investigation.

Luckily for me, I spotted Finn's car in the parking lot and knew he was in his office. I parked on the street in front of the building and hurried inside.

"Careful on the driving today," Finn cautioned. "The roads are as icy as I've ever seen them."

"Yeah, I basically slid around the corner from the harbor road onto Main and I was only going five miles an hour. What I really want to do is go home and hibernate until spring, but I'm still trying to figure out what happened to Charles Pottage. Were you ever able to track down any additional reports that might have been filed after the one I have a copy of?"

"There wasn't a lot, but yeah, I found a few things. I was actually going to call you today."

"Well, here I am, saving you the trouble. What did you find?"

Finn sorted through the files on his desk. He pulled one out of the middle of the pile and opened it.

"Tripp Brimmer was the deputy who first responded and this is the original report Balthazar Pottage gave you a copy of. There were a couple of other reports generated after that, which I don't believe you have. One was filed by the sheriff at the time, a man named Bud Brown. He came to many of the same conclusions Tripp did, but he seemed to think Belle Pottage knew something she wasn't saying."

"Like what?" I asked. It didn't make sense that Belle would hold anything back. Her baby was missing; what motivation could she possibly have to hide anything?

"I don't know. Bud never found out. She died the day after he interviewed her."

Okay, that was news, although I wasn't sure what I could do with it.

"The second report I found was from an FBI agent. He interviewed Belle on the same day as Bud. Apparently there was an anonymous call informing the agency that a baby fitting the description of

Charles was spotted in Seattle four days after the kidnapping. The FBI agent came to the island to check out the situation in response to the lead, but nothing ever came of it."

"Do you think that baby could have been Charles?" I wondered. "If it was him that would prove someone managed to get him off the island."

"I don't know. The person who called in the tip described the outfit Baby Charles was wearing when he disappeared and his description of his coloring and features were similar, but a photo of the baby had been all over the news, so it could have been a hoax."

"Okay, so an anonymous caller phones in a tip that results in a visit from an FBI agent. Later that day Bud interviews Belle and he comes away with the feeling she's holding something back. Belle leaves the house in the middle of a storm the very next day. Do you think the tip and her plan to leave the island are related?"

"Maybe. I have no way of knowing what was going through the woman's mind, but if I had to guess I'd say they were related. Maybe she received a ransom demand and was told not to tell anyone else or the baby would die. I'm not sure we'll ever know for certain."

I sat back and looked out the window at the dark sky. Not knowing what occurred wasn't an option if I was going to save the Bayview Apartments.

"I'm going to head over to talk to Tripp," I informed Finn. "I'm not sure he knows anything relevant that he didn't include in his report, but it won't hurt to ask. Maybe talking about it will jog a memory he isn't even aware he has."

"Be careful navigating the roads."

"I will. If you think of anything else text me."

I left Finn's office and headed north. Tripp Brimmer lived in an old oceanfront home just outside of Harthaven. Although the trip would normally have taken all of ten minutes, with the icy roads and the need for caution it took me thirty. Maybe, I decided after I pulled up in front of the dark house, I should have called first. I went up to the door and knocked just to be certain he really wasn't at home, but no one answered.

I returned to my car and called Tara, who reported that she and Alex were fine on their own until the arrival of the next ferry. I still had a couple of hours, so I decided to see if I could track down Roger Riverton, the man who'd been hired to guard the staircase leading to the second story of the Pottage home. Fortunately, he still lived on the island and still had the same phone number that was on the sheriff's report. He told me he was heading out for an early lunch, and I arranged to meet him at the Driftwood Café.

"Good morning, Molly," I greeted the cashier as I walked into the warm and wonderful-smelling restaurant. "I love what you did with your window."

"Thanks. I think it turned out well. I had that old train set from when my kids were little and figured it would make for a festive Christmas scene. Can I get you a table?"

"I'm meeting a man named Roger Riverton."

"He's in the back. He always sits in the booth in the corner by the window."

"Thanks. I'll find him."

I took an appreciative breath of the wonderful aromas coming from the kitchen as I walked to the back of the restaurant, where a middle-aged man was nursing a cup of coffee. It was too bad I didn't have time to stay for lunch. My stomach was beginning to rumble at the thought of one of the hot turkey sandwiches I'd noticed were on special that day.

"Mr. Riverton?" I asked as I approached the man in the booth.

"You can call me Roger."

"I'm Cait Hart."

"Figured."

I sat down across from him.

I decided it was best to jump right in. "As I explained on the phone, I'm looking into Charles Pottage's kidnapping as sort of a favor to Balthazar Pottage."

"The old curmudgeon doesn't deserve to have a pretty girl like you wasting your time on a problem he brought on himself," the man responded.

"What do you mean?" I nodded in the affirmative when a waitress asked if I wanted coffee.

"The old miser made a living off the misfortune of others," Roger answered. "I'm not a bit surprised someone decided to enact their revenge. Of course I did feel bad for the missus. She was a sweet woman who didn't deserve to have her baby taken from her."

"Did you work for Mr. Pottage on a regular basis or were you just brought in for the day?" I asked.

"I usually worked the front gate. There were a few of us who traded off so that coverage would be available around the clock. Mr. Pottage asked me to work inside on the day of the christening, but normally there wasn't a guard posted inside the house."

"Did it seem odd to you that Mr. Pottage wanted a guard inside the house on that day? It seems like everyone who was invited was a friend or family member."

"Not really." Roger shrugged. "Mr. Pottage didn't even want to have the christening. It seemed like he'd been concerned about a specific threat ever since the baby was born. Mrs. Pottage, however, insisted on the christening and even arranged for her out-of-town guests to arrive while her husband was away on business. When he came home early and found them in the house he was furious. I got the feeling that he felt threatened by one or more of the guests. He told all the guys at the gatehouse that neither Mrs. Pottage nor Baby Charles were to leave the estate unless accompanied by him. It was almost like he knew something was going to happen before it did."

I frowned. I really was anxious to speak to Balthazar Pottage again. It looked like there were things going on he hadn't shared with me. I wished I could make the trip before Monday, but Friday and Saturday were going to be busy at the bookstore and my mom would have a fit if I didn't show up for dinner on Sunday.

"On the day of the christening, who went up to the second story of the house?"

"Just Mrs. Pottage. The nanny, a nice woman named Edith Cribbage, was upstairs the entire time. She never went downstairs until after Baby Charles was found to be missing and the deputy came and questioned everyone. Mrs. Pottage went upstairs to put Charles down for a nap and then went back upstairs a while later to check on him. I asked how the baby was doing and she said he was sleeping peacefully. When Mrs. Pottage returned a third time, maybe an hour later, the baby was missing. I know there are folks who assume the kidnapper must have gotten past me, but I swear to you, I never left my post."

"What about Mr. Pottage? Did he go upstairs at all during the day?"

"No. Just the missus."

I paused to consider the timeline. All of the guests were present during the christening. Shortly after the ceremony Belle took Charles upstairs for a nap. She came down a short time later to rejoin the party.

"Do you remember when Father Kilian left?" I asked.

"Shortly after the missus put the baby to bed. When she went back downstairs he said his good-byes and left."

"And the mayor and his wife?"

"Shortly after the priest."

"Did anyone else leave during that time span?" I wondered. Anyone who left prior to Belle going up to check on Charles the first time could be taken off the suspect list because he was still sleeping peacefully at that point.

"The catering lady. I know that because the cook brought me a plate after she took over. I don't believe anyone else left before Mrs. Pottage went up to check on the baby for the first time."

So everyone else could be the kidnapper. The problem was that no one seemed a likely candidate.

"Is there anything else you can remember that might help me?"

The man shrugged. "Nothing that comes to mind."

"Okay, well, thank you for taking the time to speak to me. If you think of anything else will you call me?"

"The old geezer doesn't deserve your help."

"I know, but he's promised to rescind the eviction notices that were issued for the Bayview Apartments and allow the residents to stay permanently if I help him find his son."

Roger frowned. "Well, I guess that's as good a reason as any to help the old man. If I think of anything I'll call you."

Chapter 8

"Can I have your attention?" I called as Cody, Tara, the kids from the St. Patrick's children's choir, and I gathered in the choir room for our first of two dress rehearsals. The kids were super amped up about the fact that they were able to wear the costumes they'd been assigned for the play, leading to an increased level of noise and activity.

"We have exactly six days until we're scheduled to perform in front of all of your families and friends, so we need to be sure we get this right. I need you all to pay close attention to what Cody, Tara, and I tell you."

"How come we can't use a real baby for baby Jesus?" Trinity asked. She looked angelic in her cute white angel costume, but her whininess and cranky disposition that day had me thinking the role had been miscast.

"Because real babies cry and we wouldn't want to have the play interrupted. Besides, I don't think I know anyone with a baby small enough."

"Maybe Destiny will have her baby early and we can use him," Trinity insisted. "It's going to look so fake if we have a baby Jesus that doesn't even move."

"I don't think using Destiny's baby is going to work out," I answered. "She isn't due until after Christmas."

"Maybe we can ask Destiny if she can have the baby sooner."

"It doesn't work that way. The doll will be fine."

"But if the baby is in the play she can't give it away," Trinity insisted.

Ah. I thought I'd just stumbled across the source of Trinity's disagreeable disposition.

I knelt down so that we were face to face. "Are you worried about Destiny's baby?"

"My mom said he might have to go to another family. I don't want him to go. I want to be an aunt. I'll be a good aunt. My mom said it's going to be hard for Destiny to take care of a baby on her own, but I can help. I keep telling everyone I can help, but nobody is listening."

"It's frustrating when people don't take you seriously," I agreed.

"People shouldn't give their kids away. It isn't right."

I took a deep breath. The situation was so very complicated and now wasn't the right time to have this conversation with the eight-year-old.

"I can see that you're very concerned about this," I tried. "And I think that as the baby's aunt you should definitely be able to talk about your feelings and concerns. I'm afraid that now isn't the best time, though. Maybe you and I can go for ice cream this weekend and talk about the situation for as long as you want."

Trinity hesitated.

"Maybe on Saturday. I plan to come to the church dinner and I know your mom will be bringing you as well. Maybe you and I can sneak away after."

"Okay." I could tell Trinity wasn't totally sold on the idea, but she seemed to be willing to go along with it.

"So you're okay for tonight?" I asked.

"Yeah. I'm okay."

"Wonderful. Now hurry over and join the other angels."

I stood up and looked at the list in my hand. "Okay, let's get back to work. It seems the angels are set, so how about the barn animals? Matthew, did you ask your mom if we could use your dog?"

"She said it's fine. We can dress him like a donkey, but she doesn't want anyone to actually sit on him."

"No, of course not." Matthew's dog was a well-behaved Great Dane that would make a fine donkey for Joseph, who was being played by Matthew, to lead to the manger.

"And what about using a couple of your dogs?" I asked Samantha. Her mom bred midsize terriers. They were fluffy and white and I figured they looked as close to sheep as we were likely to get.

"She said it will be fine to use them, but she does recommend that you keep them on leashes."

"I planned to assign the shepherds to escort them in. Are there any questions?"

That, I should have realized, was the wrong thing to ask because almost everyone had a question and very few of them were relevant to the play. It took several minutes to answer everyone's inquiry, but eventually we were ready to begin.

"Okay; we're going to walk in a straight line down the hall and line up at the back of the stage. On the night of the play there'll be a curtain that we'll line up behind, but for now we'll just pretend there's a curtain. Annabelle and the angels will begin the first hymn as Joseph, Mary, and the donkey walk slowly onto the center of the stage. Joseph will say his lines and then continue on with Mary toward the opposite side of the stage. The shepherds and their sheep will enter as the narrator sets the scene."

Thankfully, everyone did as they were instructed, and other than the fact that a couple of the shepherds decided to engage in a wrestling match halfway through the reading of the birth of Christ, the rehearsal actually went pretty well.

"Okay, everyone, remember, we'll be presenting our Christmas concert on Sunday during the regular Mass, we'll have another dress rehearsal for the play on Tuesday, and the performance of the play will be on Wednesday evening," I announced after the rehearsal was over. "We have two very important events to prepare for. It's important that everyone shows up and everyone is on time. I have a sheet of instructions that I need each of you to give to your parents. Don't forget."

I let out a sigh of relief as the kids filed out to the reception area, where their parents were waiting. Maybe we'd get through this busy holiday season after all.

"That went well," Tara said when she joined me near the piano, where I was assembling the sheet music we'd need for Sunday's concert.

"Yeah. I think it went better than expected. I almost wish it hadn't."

"Why would you say that?"

"I just figure that if the rehearsals go too smoothly the actual performance is bound to be a disaster. We have over twenty kids participating. Something is sure to go wrong and I'd just as soon it happen at rehearsal and not on the night of the play."

Tara laughed. "Look at you being the worrywart. That's supposed to be my role."

I smiled. "You're right. What was I thinking?"

"I guess I should get home to Destiny."

"I spoke to Trinity. She's really upset about the fact that Destiny might give up her baby. She told me that she wants to be an aunt, and she doesn't think moms should give away their babies. You and I know it's a lot more complicated than that, but the poor thing is really sad. I told her I'd take her for ice cream on Saturday so we can talk about it, but I honestly have no idea what I'll say to her. I almost feel like we should invite Destiny to come with us."

"I wouldn't do that," Tara advised. "Just listen to what Trinity has to say and let her know you understand her concerns. I doubt there's anything you can say that's going to make this easier on her. Destiny has a hard choice to make, and whatever she decides to do, it's going to affect a lot of people and she knows it. She's stressed enough over the whole thing without throwing in the fact that her sister is so upset."

"Yeah, you're right. I'll handle it the best I can. Thanks for the advice."

Tara squeezed my arm. "I'm happy to help. Tomorrow should be busy at the store. You'll be on time?"

"I will," I promised.

"I figure this is our last big weekend before the holiday. We may as well try to make the best of it. I even hired a group of carolers to perform in front of the store when the ferry debarks, and Alex has agreed to play Santa on Friday and Saturday. He's going to wear the costume the church rented for him to use at the dinner on Saturday night."

"That's a great idea. Alex really is working out well. I'm very grateful to Ebenezer for bringing him to us, although so far the silly cat hasn't done a lot to help me figure out what happened to Charles Pottage."

"He will." Tara hugged me. "See you tomorrow, and remember, don't be late."

I finished sorting the music while I waited for Cody, who was in the reception area with the kids, waiting until each and every child was picked up. It seemed like every week there was at least one parent lagging, making us wait for them.

"Long day?" Cody asked when he was finished.

"Yeah. I think my brain is just exhausted from trying to figure out how Charles Pottage disappeared into thin air because as far as I can tell that's exactly what happened. He was upstairs when he was taken and no one other than his mama went up or down the stairs. It makes no sense."

"I agree, but something did happen to the baby, and unless he was abducted by aliens who beamed him up from his crib to their spaceship, I'm going to go out on a limb and say there's an explanation even if we don't see it right now."

I frowned. "I hadn't thought about the spaceship angle."

"I was kidding," Cody assured me.

"It's an explanation that makes sense, though."

"No, it doesn't. I think I'd better feed you before you slip completely into delirium. How does Italian sound?"

"Perfect."

Antonio's was a local favorite. I was almost weaned on Antonio's spaghetti and meatballs. My mouth began to water as we neared the brightly lit restaurant. I hadn't stopped to think about it, but I realized I hadn't paused to eat all day. The smell of garlic in the air was making my stomach rumble a bit more loudly than was appropriate.

"Oh, look, there's Finn and Siobhan." I waved to my sister. She gestured us over.

"We just sat down," Siobhan said. "We haven't ordered yet. Join us."

I looked at Cody. He nodded, so I took the chair closest to Siobhan and Cody sat down across from me.

"How was rehearsal?" Siobhan asked.

Cody and I spent the next fifteen minutes filling her in on the good, the bad, and the downright ugly.

"I can't wait for Wednesday," Siobhan commented. "It sounds like it's going to be adorable. I didn't really do much to celebrate the holidays when I lived in Seattle. I find that I'm enjoying every little thing about the holiday this year. I even helped Maggie decorate her tree."

"I'm so glad you're home. I always felt bad that you weren't with us after you moved away."

The waitress came over to take our orders, effectively pausing the conversation. I had a hard time deciding because everything was so good but eventually decided on the lasagna.

"How's everything in the land of local politics?" I asked after the waitress left to get our salads.

"Pretty good, although that developer who was all set to buy the Bayview Apartments land is pretty mad. He's crying foul and insisting that you interfered in his business deal. He's threatening all sorts of nasty things, but personally, I don't think he has a leg to stand on. Still, I'd watch my back if I were you."

I frowned. "I wasn't trying to mess up his deal. I was just trying to save the building."

"I know that and you know that, but this guy is a real jerk. He had an oral agreement to buy the land from Balthazar Pottage after he evicted the tenants and tore down the building, but as far as I can tell there was nothing in writing. The man is furious, but I don't think he has any grounds to legally do anything about the fact that Pottage changed his mind. You should be aware that he's most likely working on Pottage as we speak, and you don't have anything in writing either. I'm just hoping the old guy will honor his commitment to you and not let the developer strong-arm him into changing his mind once again."

"I guess I'd better wrap this thing up and get something in writing from Pottage before the developer gets in the middle of things."

"Have you made any progress since we last spoke?" Finn asked.

"Not really."

I spent the entire time we were eating our salad filling him in on everything I'd learned that day and the conclusions, or lack thereof, that I'd come to.

"I have to say I'm leaning toward Cody's alien abduction theory," I concluded as our entrées were set in front of us.

"Either someone is lying or maybe everyone is lying," Finn commented. "Something happened to the child and I don't think it was aliens."

"Who do you still need to talk to?" Siobhan asked.

"Tripp Brimmer, Jane Partridge, who was working for the Pottages as a maid, Liza Bolton the cook, and Edith Cribbage the nanny. There were also some out-of-town friends and relatives I haven't tried to track down. I hoped I could figure this out by simply interviewing the people who are available locally."

"I have to agree with Finn," Siobhan said. "Something happened to that baby. The fact that it seems impossible that he was taken from his room can only mean that one of the key players is lying."

"Key players?" I asked.

"The nanny or the upstairs guard or both come to mind."

"Yeah, it does seem likely that one or both were in on it. I guess I'll just have to see what the nanny has to say."

"I have a meeting with the sheriff tomorrow about a recent assault case; if you haven't figured this out by next week I'll make some time to help you," Finn offered.

"Me too." Siobhan nodded. "The island offices are closed for two weeks beginning on Monday."

"Thanks, guys. I think I might end up needing everyone's help with this one."

Chapter 9

Friday, December 18

As promised, I was not only on time at work the following day but I was three minutes early. Yes, I realize three minutes doesn't really earn me bragging rights, but given the fact that I'm almost always late, it felt like quite a victory.

Apparently, Tara thought so as well because she gave me a huge smile when I walked through the front door. It was obvious she had arrived much earlier than I; holiday music was playing in the background, the tree lights and the lights we'd strung around the store were all turned on, and there was coffee waiting for me on the counter.

"I have good news," Tara informed me. "I stopped by that new restaurant in the harbor on my way home last night to pick up some takeout and realized the name of the woman who rang me up was Liza Bolton. I asked if she used to work for Balthazar Pottage and she said she had. I explained that you were trying to help locate his son and she said she'd be happy to stop by the bookstore today if we were willing to buy her a cup of coffee. So see, you can sleuth without even having to leave the building."

"That's great. Thanks. I do want to speak to her. Did she say what time she'd be here?"

"Around eleven, which is between ferries, so it's a good time for us."

"Perfect. Is Alex here?"

"He's in the office inputting the new inventory that came over on last night's ferry into the computer. He really is a great employee. And he's so good with the kids. I've already asked him about working for us over the summer and he seemed open to the idea."

"That'd be great. And he's such a good sport. There aren't many twenty-year-old guys who would be willing to put on a Santa suit for the kids."

"Marva from the church delivered it this morning. I'm superexcited to see whether having Santa available for photos will bring in additional foot traffic. I've posted a notice that Santa will be here from two until five this afternoon."

"Perfect. I'll finish helping you shelve the new inventory as soon as I get the cats settled. Hopefully,

Liza will be on time and we can chat before it gets too busy."

As it turned out, not only did Liza show up right on time but she brought Jane Partridge, the Pottages' maid, with her. It wasn't superbusy during the morning hours, but there was a steady flow of customers, so Liza, Jane, and I took our coffee into the cat lounge.

"I've been wanting to stop in to check out your place," Jane said. "I love cats and coffee."

"Please come by any time. We have cats on site every day to visit with while you sip your coffee and enjoy a book."

"So you're looking into the disappearance of Charles Pottage," Liza commented. It appeared that, unlike her friend, she wasn't there for chitchat.

I nodded.

"Why? It's been twenty years. What can you possibly hope to learn after twenty years?"

I explained about my agreement with Pottage concerning the apartment building and my real motive behind wanting to solve the case.

"I can respect that," Liza said. "I know a couple of people who live in that building. How can I help?"

"I'd just like each of you to tell me what you remember about that day."

The women shared their memories, and it was clear they both remembered things much the same way everyone else had. There had been tension between Belle and Balthazar Pottage that had been building for some time. The much older man treated his wife like a prisoner most of the time. He told everyone it was to protect her, but both women felt it was really more about controlling her. They remembered that Mr. Pottage had been furious about the guests Belle had invited, and he'd insisted that they be given bedrooms on the first floor and told not to venture to the second floor at any time. They also reported that the couple had been sleeping in separate rooms ever since Charles was born. Of course Charles had been kidnapped when he was only six weeks old, so the fact that Belle had recently given birth might have had something to do with the sleeping arrangements.

Although she'd been hired as a maid, Jane had spent the day of the christening helping with the buffet lunch because the woman who'd handled the catering had to leave. Liza had spent the day in the same way. Both women had gone back and forth from the kitchen to the area where the buffet had been set up and both insisted they hadn't noticed anything odd.

"Do either of you know who the caterer was?" I asked.

"No," Liza answered. "If you ask me it was a total waste of money to hire a caterer when I could have come up with something just as nice."

"Why *did* the Pottages have the luncheon catered?" I asked.

"I have no idea." Liza shrugged. "The missus and I got along well and she seemed to like my cooking, but she was most insistent that the affair be catered by this woman. I think she might have been friends with her. I saw them speaking several times before the guests arrived."

"But she left shortly after the ceremony was over?" I verified.

"Yeah. She said she had another event she needed to get to. She left shortly after the mayor and his wife did."

I felt like there was a clue there, but for the life of me I didn't know what it was. The timeline seemed to be airtight; everyone seemed in agreement as to who was where at what time. If everyone was telling the truth Baby Charles couldn't have been taken from the house. Yet somehow he had been.

"Do you mind if I go over this one more time?" I asked the women.

"Feel free," Jane answered.

"The christening was Mrs. Pottage's idea."

"Yes."

"And the overnight guests showed up while Mr. Pottage was out of town."

"Correct."

"And Mr. Pottage was angry when he found out about the guests and the christening in general?"

"He was."

"On the day of the christening the caterer showed up first?"

"She did but only just a few minutes prior to Father Kilian's arrival," Jane informed me.

"And the local guests showed up at some point following the arrival of Father Kilian."

The women nodded.

"What time was the ceremony?"

"One o'clock," Liza answered.

"And what time was it over?"

"About one fifteen. The missus took the baby upstairs to put him down immediately after Father Kilian completed the service."

"And what time did Father Kilian leave?"

The women looked at each other. "I guess around one thirty, maybe one forty-five," Jane answered. "It's hard to remember exactly, but I remember he said his good-byes to Mrs. Pottage as soon as she came down from tending to the baby."

"And the caterer? When did she leave?"

"Shortly after. The mayor and his wife also left, but everyone else stayed to eat," Liza reconfirmed what I'd already been told by others.

"And then Mrs. Pottage went upstairs again?"

"So we heard," Jane answered. "We were busy in the kitchen and didn't see Mrs. Pottage go upstairs to check on the baby. It was Roger, the man who was guarding the stairs, who told us that she went back upstairs—probably at around two o'clock, give or take a few minutes, and she told him the baby was sleeping peacefully and returned to the party. She didn't find him missing until later, around three o'clock."

"Why do you think it was Mrs. Pottage and not the nanny who was attending to Charles, given the fact that there was company in the house?" I asked.

"The nanny—a woman named Edith Cribbage—hadn't been feeling well. Charles was a fussy baby and I don't think she was getting enough sleep," Jane informed me. "I've heard people say she fell asleep on the day of the kidnapping, but it's always bothered me that the baby was taken while she slept in the next room. She was a trained nanny and was used to sleeping with one eye open. I'm certain she would have heard the baby had he wakened and cried."

"Okay, thank you I guess that's all I need for now. Please do let me know if you think of anything else."

While both women had seemed nice enough, neither of them had told me anything I hadn't already known. I did, however, learn that Edith Cribbage lived on San Juan Island. Maybe I'd stop there and try to speak to her on my way out to Balthazar Pottage's estate on Monday.

"So?" Tara asked after the women had left.

"I got a phone number for the nanny, but other than that, they said pretty much the same thing everyone else has. I still need to talk to Tripp, which I may try to do when I get off here. Other than that, I guess I'll just have to wait to hear what Pottage has to say about things when I visit him next week. The people I've talked to have given me an entirely different perspective on his relationship with his wife than he led me to believe when I spoke to him on Monday. It sounds to me like he almost anticipated what would happen."

"It does seem like he suspected his son was in danger, given all the precautions he took. Maybe he can shed some light on the source of the threat. It might end up tying in."

"I hope so. I also need to talk to him about the developer he was working with before we made our deal."

I filled Tara in on my conversation with Siobhan the previous evening.

"That's crazy."

"Tell me about it," I agreed. "All I'm trying to do is to help my neighbors remain in their homes and suddenly I'm on this guy's hit list."

"He doesn't sound like the sort of person we want on the island anyway. I for one think we should find a way to keep him from building here no matter how things work out with the Bayview Apartments."

"I couldn't agree more."

Tara looked over toward the front door of the store. "It looks like you have a visitor."

I turned around to see Ebenezer standing outside the door. I wanted to ask how he'd gotten there as I let him in, but then realized if he could get from Balthazar Pottage's island to Madrona Island, he would certainly have no problem getting from my cabin to the bookstore.

"I don't know why you're here, but I have to work to do, so whatever you have in mind will have to wait," I said to the cat.

He just looked at me, then trotted over to the door that separated the cat lounge from the coffee bar. I opened the door and he trotted inside. He headed to the sofa, where he curled up in a ball and went to sleep.

"I guess he just didn't want to stay home alone," I decided. "Max is with Cody today."

"He really is a beautiful cat. I hope we won't have anyone wanting to adopt him."

That very situation was the reason I'd never brought the cats Tansy sent to work with me to the store. Each and every one of them was gorgeous and would have generated a lot of interest as a potential adoptee.

"Maybe I should put a *sold* sign around his neck," I teased.

"Hopefully he'll reveal whatever it is he's here for during the lull between the midday ferry and the last ferry of the day," Tara commented. "I anticipate both will be filled close to capacity with the holiday next week."

As it turned out, Ebenezer didn't seem to have any plans for me but rather for a boy who was four years of age and terrified of animals. He came in with his mom and started to totally freak out when he saw the cats. The mother apologized and shared with Tara and me that her son was deathly afraid of all animals and she had no idea why. She'd brought him into the store in the hope that he'd be willing to at least look at the cats through the glass. She was afraid his intense fear of animals was stunting his social development because he refused to go anywhere animals might be present, which was pretty much everywhere.

The woman explained that she'd taken the boy to see a psychologist, who couldn't figure out what the problem might be. As far as the mom knew, the child had never been bitten by a dog or harmed by any other type of animal. She really had no idea where his fear came from. Tara invited her to have a cup of coffee while the child played nearby with the blocks we provide for our youngest guests. I don't know how he did it, but Ebenezer somehow managed to make his way from the cat lounge into the coffee bar. I was about to make a mad dash to intercept him when I noticed the little boy smiling at him. Tara and his mother were intent on their conversation and hadn't yet noticed, and I decided to wait while the drama played out.

Ebenezer slowly walked over to the child and lay down next to him. The boy slowly reached out a hand and touched the cat on the stomach. I held my breath; he momentarily looked like he was going to cry before tossing the blocks aside and paying full attention to the cat. He didn't seem to be aware that I was watching, and Tara and the mom still hadn't noticed, so I made my way slowly over to the coffee bar in the hope of intercepting them before either made a big deal over what was occurring.

"Don't look up and don't turn around," I whispered, "but your son is petting one of the cats."

The mom's eyes grew big. "Really?"

"Yeah. But don't make a big deal out of it. That can only backfire. Slowly turn around and smile, but then go back to your conversation as if nothing of any importance is happening."

The woman did as I suggested, but the child was so intent on the cat that he didn't seem to notice.

"That's amazing," the woman whispered. "How did you do that?"

"I didn't do anything. Ebenezer did it all by himself."

"I want to adopt that cat," the woman announced.

"I'm sorry," I apologized, "he isn't one of my cats. He belongs to a friend of mine. I'm only keeping him for a short time."

"Oh, that's too bad." The woman looked disappointed, and given the circumstances, I couldn't blame her.

"If you want to bring your son back tomorrow I'll have Ebenezer here. Maybe we can work together to help your son choose another cat. I'll bring in some of my most kickback kitties."

"It's worth a try. His fear of animals seemed to have appeared instantly overnight; maybe he can get over it just as abruptly."

"We can let your son play with Ebenezer a little while longer. We really aren't supposed to have the cats in the coffee bar, but hopefully no one will complain. We should move him before the ferry docks and the crowd comes in, though."

The child continued to play with Ebenezer until we saw the ferry on the horizon. The mom casually told the child it was time to leave but that they could come back the next day if he wanted. He smiled, said okay, and left without a fuss.

I picked up Ebenezer and looked him in the eye. "You really are a magical cat, aren't you?"

The cat didn't answer, but he did start to purr. Loudly. I cuddled him to my chest and scratched him behind the ear. He really was a sweetie. I was willing to bet he provided a lot of companionship for Balthazar Pottage despite the fact that the old man pretended not to care about him one way or the other.

I took Ebenezer to the cat lounge and then headed into the back room to let Alex know that the arrival of Santa to the bookstore was less than a half hour away, so he might want to get ready. He'd already donned the suit but was having problems with the white wig and long beard. I volunteered to help him.

"Hold still," I said as I tied his long dark hair back in a band so it wouldn't show beneath the wig.

"I'm trying to, but that tickles."

"Don't be a baby. I'm just brushing your hair. There." I stood back to admire my handiwork. "I think I've got everything tucked up. Now for the wig."

"I hope it isn't going to be itchy," Alex complained.

"It won't be itchy," I promised, even though I had no idea if it would be or not. "We'll need to smooth back your bangs or they'll show."

Alex used his hand to smooth back the hair from his forehead.

"Interesting birthmark."

Alex had a red mark shaped like a heart on his forehead just above his left eye.

"Hence the long hair," he said.

"I don't know," I countered as I adjusted the wig so it was straight. "I kind of like it. It's got a sexy vibe to it. If I were you, I'd cut my hair and wear it proudly."

"Are you flirting with me?" Alex's eyes twinkled, which let me know he was just messing with me, but I couldn't help but turn just a tad red.

"I'm most certainly not flirting with you. I have a boyfriend."

"I know; I'm just teasing. I've always hated that birthmark, so I've always worn my hair long to cover it up. Luckily, I have thick hair that actually looks good long."

"Well, I like it, and I think other girls would too. I wasn't kidding about cutting your bangs. They look good the way they are, but I think you'd look good with your hair short as well. Are you ready?" I asked when the beard was in place.

"As I'll ever be. Let's hope we don't have any pants wetters in the crowd."

I laughed. "Yeah, let's hope."

Chapter 10

"Are you sure about this?" Cody asked me that evening as he held up a bright green sweater. Cody wanted to buy Christmas gifts for my family and had asked me to go shopping with him to help him pick out the items I felt my relatives would like best.

"Cassie will love it."

"But I thought she was into the whole black and white thing."

"She was. She's over it. Now it's loud and bright all the time."

Cody shrugged. "If you say so."

I began sorting through the sweaters to see if I could find something a bit less trendy for Siobhan, while Cody added Cassie's sweater to his basket. If we had time maybe I'd look for something for my mom and my other siblings. I was usually a lot more on the ball, but this year I'd barely even started my shopping. Still, it was fun shopping with Cody, although the heater in the store was turned up to something just short of inferno.

"Maybe we should walk down to the sporting goods store to look for something for Aiden and Danny," I suggested.

"Hot in that thick turtleneck?"

"I feel almost charbroiled."

Cody looked toward the cash registers in the front of the store. I followed his gaze. The lines were endless, as was to be expected a week before Christmas.

"Why don't you go ahead and get some fresh air? I'll pay for the stuff we picked out and meet you outside the store."

I could feel a trail of sweat trickling down my back. "Thanks. I think I'll do that. This sweater is great for the walking-around part but not so great for the actual shopping part of our outing. Maybe I should go home to change before we go to dinner. It's likely to be warm in the restaurant."

"We can do whatever you'd like," Cody assured me.

I pushed my way through the crowd as I made my way toward the exit, which wasn't an easy feat. The place was packed. The bookstore had been busy as well, but not nearly as much as the shops in town.

Coffee Cat Books closed at five on Friday, but I couldn't help but wonder if we might want to stay open later during the holidays. It was a little late to change things this year, but it would be something to keep in mind for next year.

"I see you decided to escape the heat as well," Angel Haven said to me as she exited the store shortly after I did.

"It has to be ninety degrees in there," I said to my pregnant friend after hugging her hello.

"I really don't know why they have the heat up so high. It seems like a total waste of energy, for one thing. For another, I'm going to bet we aren't the only ones to decide to leave before we were done shopping. I bet the store is actually losing a lot of money."

I glanced toward the front door, where a Salvation Army volunteer was chatting with two women who also were complaining about the heat. It seemed Angel had a point. There most likely were patrons who would have shopped longer if the temperature inside the store had been more agreeable.

"I noticed Mrs. Jasper is working the counter," I commented. "It seems that poor old dear is cold even when it's ninety degrees. Chances are she's the one who set the thermostat. Is Jesse still inside?"

"Yeah, he's paying for the stuff we picked out. I had no idea how much it was going to cost to outfit a baby. All I can say is that I'm so grateful to you for convincing Mr. Pottage to change his mind about tearing down the apartment building. You're a true hero. The building is old and run down, but it's home." Angel rubbed her big belly in a circular motion.

"I haven't convinced him yet," I clarified. "I'm trying, but it's still a long shot."

Angel pushed her hands into her back. "I know it's not a done deal," Angel said, "but you're so good at persuading people to do stuff. I'm sure you'll figure out a way. I don't know what we're going to do if we have to move. Where will we go? Before you got the old man to delay the evictions I was seriously beginning to fear I was going to have to have my baby in someone's barn, just like in the Christmas story."

I took Angel's arm and moved her to the side as two boys on bikes went barreling down the sidewalk. "I can't promise what Mr. Pottage will do in the long run, but I'll try my very hardest to convince him to find a solution that will allow the tenants to stay. I'm working on a project for him that seems to be going nowhere, so prayers would be appreciated."

"You've got it." Angel hugged me again. "And thank you. I know you'll try your hardest."

Suddenly, I felt burdened with a huge responsibility. Twelve families were counting on me to do the impossible. Oh, no, I hadn't bitten off more than I could chew. I was running out of leads, but I still had a few people to talk to, so maybe something would pop soon.

"I ran into Destiny at the doctor's office yesterday." Angel changed the subject. She'd probably noticed the panic on my face. "Did you know we're due on the same date?"

"No, I didn't realize."

"Chances are we won't actually deliver on the same day, but I thought it was cool that the possibility existed. She's having a boy and I'm having a girl. Maybe they'll share the hospital nursery, grow up friends, fall in love, and have babies of their own."

I laughed. "Boy, you like to jump ahead."

Angel smiled. "Everyone loves a love story."

I almost mentioned that Destiny was most likely going to give her baby up for adoption, but I wasn't sure she wanted anyone to know what she was considering.

"Even their names go together," Angel added.

"Names?"

"I'm naming my baby Jordan and she's naming hers James. James and Jordan; how cute is that?"

I hadn't been aware that Destiny had picked out a name. Maybe she was leaning toward keeping the baby after all. She certainly had been putting off signing the paperwork the adoption agency had given her.

"We're all set," Cody said as he came out of the store with Jesse beside him.

"It was good talking to you." I hugged Angel one last time, then looked at Jesse. "Text me when the baby comes."

"I will. It won't be long now."

Jesse put his arm around his wife and they walked away together. They looked so happy. If it were me having a baby I'd probably be more terrified than excited.

"I can't believe Angel is going to be a mother," I commented. "She's the same age I am."

"Twenty-six isn't really all that young to have a baby," Cody pointed out.

"Yeah, I guess not. It just seems so strange that the girls I grew up with are all getting married and having families. Tara and I are the last two in the group we hung out with in high school who are still single and childless."

"I guess it must be different for guys. Of the ten or so guys Danny and I hung out with the most in school only one is married and we're two years older than you."

I frowned. "I guess you have a point. Angel is twenty-six, but Jesse is thirty-two, and my friend Reina just married a man who was thirty-five last summer."

"Does it bother you?" Cody asked.

"Does what bother me?"

"That all your friends are getting married."

I thought about it. "No, not really. I think Tara is starting to think about having a family, but I feel like I'm still trying to figure out my life. I know I'll want a family one day, but at this point I'm happy with the way things are." I looked at Cody. "How about you? Is your biological clock ticking?" I teased.

Cody looked me in the eye. "Maybe a little."

Maybe a little? What did he mean by that? Was Cody ready to settle down and have babies? I knew I wasn't, so I decided I wasn't going to ask a question I might not want to hear the answer to.

"I feel a lot better now that I'm out of that oven of a store," I said as we walked toward the car. "I think what I have on will be fine for dinner. Maybe after we eat we can go up to Lookout Point to see the lights."

"That sounds nice. One of my fondest memories is of the Christmas when I was sixteen and you were fourteen and you had just had a huge fight with Siobhan, so I took you up to the Lookout in my dad's car."

I stopped walking and turned to look at Cody. "Really?"

"Yeah. It was my one big chance to play the knight in shining armor. You came to my house looking for Danny but he'd already left, so I took you up to look at the lights and we talked for hours."

I remembered every minute of that magical night, but I'd had no idea Cody remembered it too. We hadn't been dating and he certainly wasn't interested in me in a romantic way then. I'm sure all I was to him at that point was his best friend's pesky little sister.

"You really did help me put things in perspective that night. I went home and made up with Siobhan and we had a wonderful Christmas. I'm pretty sure I never even thanked you."

"You can thank me later tonight." Cody winked.

I smiled. "I might just do that."

I took Cody's hand as we continued down the street. I had always enjoyed coming downtown with my parents when I was a child to look at all the beautifully decorated windows. In a way, walking along Main Street so close to Christmas made me feel like a kid again.

I glanced at Cody. He looked so handsome in his forest green sweater. His thick dark hair was just a little long, causing it to brush his crew-neck collar. He smiled at me and suddenly I was no longer feeling like a kid. Maybe we should just skip dinner. Pick up takeout. Go back to my place so I could make good on my promise to thank him for that long-ago Christmas.

"Remind me to pick up a gift for Mr. Parsons while we are out," Cody asked, interrupting my daydream. "I thought I'd give it to him on Christmas Eve before everyone shows up for our dinner."

"By the way, I hope you don't mind, but I decided to invite Maggie and Marley to our Christmas Eve dinner. I realize we'll see them both on Christmas, but they didn't have any other plans for Christmas Eve and I thought they'd fit right in."

"That's fine," Cody answered. "I invited Father Kilian and Sister Mary as well. He has Mass at five, but he said he should be able to make it by seven, so I thought we'd just serve appetizers and then eat the main meal when he arrives."

"That sounds nice," I said as I mentally adjusted my menu to include appetizers and accommodate two more diners. "Maybe we should invite Pete Baxter. He's usually alone for the holiday and that would make an even dozen."

Pete Baxter was the local postmaster.

"That's a good idea," Cody agreed.

When we got to the car, Cody put the bags in the trunk while I checked my texts. There was one from Tara, asking me to call her. She ended the text in 911, so I did just that.

"What's up?" I asked when Tara answered on the first ring.

"It's Destiny. She's in the hospital. She slipped on the ice and fell."

"Oh, God. Is she okay?"

"She seems fine."

"And the baby?"

"They're doing some tests. Destiny is hysterical. I could really use some backup. I wanted to call her mom, but she refused to let me."

"Cody and I are on our way." I turned to him as I ended the call. "Destiny is in the hospital. We need to go there now."

Cody turned the key in the ignition. "Is she okay?" he asked as he pulled out into traffic.

"I don't know. I hope so."

Cody and I rode in silence as we made our way to the hospital. I was saying prayers the whole way and I was willing to bet Cody was doing the same.

"How is she?" I asked as soon as I rushed through the ER entrance to find Tara pacing in the waiting area. Cody had gone to find a parking space.

"I'm not sure. When we first arrived Destiny was completely hysterical. They had to give her something to calm her down. The doctor is in with her now."

I hugged Tara. I could see that she was a bundle of nerves.

"The whole time we were driving over here she kept yelling at me not to let her baby die. I'm not sure how I held it together enough to get her here, but now that she's in the doctor's capable hands I feel like I might pass out. Or throw up. Or both."

"Let's sit down." I took Tara's arm and led her to a sofa. "Cody, can you find us some water?" I asked as soon as he came in.

Tara began to cry. "She was having sharp pains in her abdomen. It totally freaked her out. It totally freaked me out."

I took a deep breath and squeezed Tara's hand. I prayed that both Destiny and her baby would be okay. I felt so helpless and I knew Tara did too.

"Maybe we *should* call her mom," I suggested.

"She said not to. I told you, I wanted to, but she made me promise."

"She's a minor," I pointed out.

"Yeah, I know. She told the doctor she was eighteen. He's new and doesn't know her, and there was so much confusion when wc came in that he didn't argue, but eventually things are going to calm down and they'll ask us to fill out additional paperwork. I guess we should call her mother."

"I'll do it," I volunteered. "That way you've kept your promise. You just sit here and take some deep breaths until the dizziness passes."

I watched the nurse behind the counter as she answered her phone and then hurried through the double doors. I had a feeling it was going to be a long night.

Chapter 11

Sunday, December 20

"My mom said Destiny is going to have her baby this week," Serenity Paulson informed me as we prepared for the Sunday morning service.

"Yes, I know. Are you excited?"

"Very. I'm going to be an aunt. Mom said I can hold Baby James when he's born. I hope he has dark hair like me."

It had been a tense night on Friday, but after all the tests were completed it was determined the baby was fine, although they'd ordered complete bedrest for Destiny until the baby was born. My sister Cassidy was out of school on Christmas break, so she'd volunteered to stay with Destiny while Tara was at work. The doctors planned to induce labor at the end of the week if she didn't deliver naturally by that time.

"I bet he'll be a beautiful baby whatever the color of his hair."

"Maybe. Destiny wants him to have dark hair too. She said his daddy's hair was blond and she doesn't want the baby to look anything like that jerk."

"She told you that?"

"No. She was talking to Jake and I overheard them. I think Destiny feels bad that James's dad doesn't want him."

"Yes," I agreed, "I'm sure it's a very emotional situation for her. Why don't you go see if Trinity needs help with her robe?"

I wasn't certain discussing Destiny's love life was appropriate for the choir room.

"Did you learn all the lines for your solo?" I asked Holly.

"Yes. My mom said it sounds real nice."

"I'm sure it does. You have a beautiful voice."

"Ms. Cait," Robby interrupted, "my robe won't zip. I think it's broken."

I joined the six-year-old. "Let me have a look."

The St. Patrick's children's choir was due to go on in less than five minutes. I really didn't have time for broken zippers. Luckily, Robby had just caught some of the fabric in the zipper when he'd put the robe on and I only needed to work it loose.

"I talked to Santa last night at the church dinner," Ricky said as I worked on Robby's robe. "I told him about the shoes and socks and he said he'd see what he could do."

"That's great," I responded. I'd already spoken to Sister Mary, who'd assured me that Santa would come through. That was one of the best things about being part of a small community; everyone looked out for everyone else.

"I asked for blue socks to go with the blue shoes I want, but if Santa doesn't have blue socks white will be fine. My mom says Santa has a lot of deliveries to make and we can't be picky."

"Your mom is right, but I'm sure Santa will try his very best to get the socks you want," I said.

I stood in the middle of the room and looked around after Ricky and Robby had walked away. On the surface there appeared to be total chaos, but I could see that everyone was working toward doing what it was they needed to do.

"Can you ask Stephanie to sing a little more quietly?" Annabelle asked as I began to pass out the hymn books. "She's singing off key and it's messing me up."

Annabelle had by far the best voice of anyone in the choir, but she also had the prickliest personality. Most of the other kids didn't really like her, which made me feel bad for her, but I had to admit she tended to bring it on herself.

"How about if I ask Cody to move you closer to the middle so you aren't right next to Stephanie?" I suggested.

"I guess that could work, though it would be better if she just moved her lips and let those of us who can actually sing do it."

"Stephanie has a nice voice. Besides, God loves to hear the voices of all His children praising Him with song."

"Maybe God is tone deaf," Annabelle grumbled as she walked away.

I looked around the festively decorated room. There was an energy and excitement in the air as the kids lined up in preparation for their journey down the hall and into the main part of the church, where Mass was being held. We planned to perform Christmas carols in place of the usual hymns. I loved everything about this season, but the thing I loved most was the joy it brought to the people around me.

"Are we ready?" Cody asked.

"Ready," all the kids responded.

"Remember, we're going to segue directly into the second song from the first without a break. Can everyone remember that?"

"Yes, Mr. Cody," everyone said.

"Okay. Everyone smile," Cody instructed as he led the group out the door.

I took up the rear to make certain everyone, including Robby, would behave themselves. I was proud of the kids. They'd worked hard and took their role in the choir very seriously. I couldn't help but predict that each and every one of them was going to grow up to be an awesome adult.

After church Cody and I went to my mom's for our weekly family dinner. Ever since I was a little girl, dinner on Sunday afternoons was mandatory for the entire Hart clan. As a teenager I wasn't fond of the time away from my friends, but as an adult I wouldn't trade the weekly event for anything.

"What time can you be here on Christmas?" my mom asked the minute I entered the kitchen.

"What time would you like me to be here?"

"Early. Maybe eight. I thought we could all have brunch before we opened presents. I'm planning on serving dinner at around three, so I figured it would be best to have brunch early in the morning."

"That sounds fine to me."

"And Cody?"

"I'm sure it will be fine with him as well. Have you checked with Danny? If anyone's going to be late it will be him."

"He's going to spend the night here. Siobhan told me eight is fine with her and Finn. I'll check with Maggie when she arrives, but she's usually an early riser."

"Can I bring Max?"

Mom hesitated.

"It's Christmas, and I'll be out for a good part of the day."

"Oh, all right, you can bring the dog."

My mom wasn't really an animal person. I'd never had a pet of my own until after I'd moved out of the house and into the cabin. Now I couldn't imagine my life without one.

"Caitlin, can you set the table?" Mom asked after delegating other chores to other members of the family.

"How many are we having?" I asked.

"Fourteen. I invited Father Kilian and Sister Mary to join the family."

"Okay, I'm on it."

I assumed the other twelve consisted of Cody and me, Aiden and his girlfriend, Danny and Tara, Siobhan and Finn, Cassie and Mom, and Maggie and Marley. Up until a few days ago Cassie's boyfriend would have attended as well, but I'd heard the pair had broken up, which I assumed explained Cassie's sour mood.

"I'm surprised Tara is here," Siobhan said as she pitched in to help me set the table. "I figured she'd be watching over Destiny."

"Destiny's mom had the day off, so she's staying with her," I explained. "Tara will be there tonight and all day tomorrow because the store is closed, and Cassie is going to sit with her on Tuesday and Wednesday while Tara's at work. If all goes as planned, she should deliver on Thursday morning."

"Thursday is Christmas Eve. Destiny will have a Christmas baby."

"It looks like it."

"I hope everything goes okay. She's just a kid."

"Yeah. I've been worried about her since the fall. She seems to be all right, but I think she fell pretty hard. Still, I guess if the doctors aren't worried I shouldn't be either."

Siobhan began setting the water glasses on the table as I worked on the silverware. It was nice to share a chore with my sister that we'd both hated when we were growing up.

"By the way," Siobhan added as we worked, "I wanted to tell you that I overheard a group of women from Tuesday night bible study talking about the situation with the Bayview Apartments. They were all praising you for saving the day."

"I really wish my persuading Balthazar Pottage to change his mind hadn't gotten out. Now I feel all this pressure to come through and I honestly don't know if I can."

Siobhan opened a drawer in the china hutch and took out a stack of cloth napkins. "Don't let the expectations of others influence your plan. Do what you feel inclined to do and let the chips fall where they may. I don't see how anyone can fault you for trying, no matter what the outcome."

"I guess, but people are looking at me as some kind of a hero and I feel like I'll be letting everyone down if I can't find Charles Pottage. For all I know he's been dead for twenty years and is therefore unfindable. You must be dealing with pressure like this every day as mayor. How do you do it?"

Siobhan stopped what she was doing and looked at me. "I do the very best I can in a given situation and then I move on. I don't beat myself up over the outcome if it isn't the one I'd hoped for. You win some and you lose some. Whatever the outcome of your crusade, just remember that you're the one who's actually *doing* something to save the apartments, while everyone else was just standing on the sidelines complaining. Win or lose, you're a hero in my eyes."

"Thanks." I straightened the flowers in the center of the table. "I needed to hear that. Have I told you lately how glad I am you moved home?"

"About a million times." Siobhan laughed.

"This is nice," I said to Cody later that evening as we shared a bottle of wine. The fire was dancing in the fireplace, the tree lights twinkled from the tree in front of the window, and the sound of Christmas piano played softly.

"I do enjoy spending Sundays with your family, but by the end of the day I'm ready for a little *us* time. My family never really did the bonding thing. I'm not used to all the drama."

"Like Cassie's breakup?"

"Exactly. I feel bad for her, but after a while I got tired of listening to her complain about the guy. To be honest I'm kind of surprised she's this upset. It never seemed like she was all that in to him while they were dating."

"I don't think she was; I just don't think she liked getting dumped."

"I guess none of us do."

I looked at Cody. "Like you've ever been dumped."

"I've been dumped."

"When?" As I recalled all the girls had loved him and he was the one doing the dumping.

"When I was in the Navy. I was in a relationship for almost two years when the woman I thought I loved decided she no longer loved me."

I frowned. I'd had no idea Cody had been in that serious of a relationship. I figured he must have dated while he was away but two years?

"I'm sorry."

Cody shrugged. "It was a long time ago, and in retrospect I realize I was never really in love with her. At least not the way I'm in love with you."

I smiled.

"I thought maybe we should go on a sleigh ride this week."

"It's been snowing, but there's only about two inches on the ground. I don't think it's enough for a sleigh," I pointed out.

"There's a man in town who provides rides with a sleigh that's been outfitted with wheels. It might not be quite the same as going for a ride when there's a lot of snow, but the sleigh follows a path through the forest on a track made from hard-packed powder. It seems like it would be romantic all the same."

"That sounds nice. I've never taken a sleigh ride. Although we have a pretty busy week. I'm planning to go visit Balthazar Pottage tomorrow, and then we have play rehearsal on Tuesday and the performance on Wednesday. Thursday is Christmas Eve and then Friday is Christmas."

Cody put his arm around me. I lay my head on his shoulder. I really loved these random moments where I felt that the two of us really were part of a whole.

Cody kissed the top of my head before he replied. "I guess Christmas did sort of sneak up on me. By the way, I'm afraid we have two more guests to add to our Christmas Eve dinner party. Mr. Parsons asked if a couple of the guys who hang out at the senior center could come and I told him it would be fine. I guess that brings us to fourteen."

"Make that sixteen. I invited Doris Rutherford because she was hanging out at the Bait and Stitch when I stopped in and Maggie asked me about bringing something. She was thrilled with the invite and wanted to know if she could bring her neighbor."

"I guess our little low-key dinner party has taken on a life of its own," Cody commented. "Initially I figured we'd have an early dinner with Mr. Parsons and then head back to your place for a little alone time. Somehow that's morphed into sixteen guests and a late dinner to accommodate Father Kilian."

"It's fine," I assured him. "It's a nice thing to do. I do wish we could have had a bit more us time, but we're alone right now."

Cody pulled me into his arms just as my phone rang. I was going to ignore it when I noticed the call was from Tara. I'd just seen her at my mom's so I had to assume this was important. I groaned at the bad timing as I pulled away and answered. "Hello?"

"It's Destiny. She's in labor. We're on our way to the hospital."

"We'll meet you there."

Chapter 12

Monday, December 21

I stood out on the exterior deck as the ferry made its way to San Juan Island. It was cold, so I was the only one outside, but I felt that I needed the fresh air to clear the cobwebs from my brain. I'd thought of bringing Ebenezer back today, but I could sense he wasn't ready to go. I hoped the interviews I had planned for the day would bring me closer to an answer about Baby Charles, but I knew deep in my gut that I hadn't yet reached the end of the line.

I'd had a long night. Destiny had delivered a healthy baby boy, but not until after she'd had to endure hours of labor. She still hadn't said she was definitely keeping James, but based on the way she'd looked at him with total adoration, I had to believe she would. Her friend Jake had been at the hospital as well, and he seemed as enamored with the baby as she was. I wasn't sure there was a future for them as a couple, but I sensed Jake would be there for Destiny as she navigated the rocky road of single parenthood, should she choose to do so.

I felt a tension in my chest as the ferry pulled into the harbor. Although I didn't think today would bring me to the end of the road I was traveling, I did feel the conversations I planned to have that day might be intense and emotional.

I'd called the nanny, Edith Cribbage, and arranged to meet with her before I headed out to the Pottage estate. She lived in a small house within walking distance from the ferry terminal. My plan was to have a chat with her and then return to the harbor, where I could rent a water taxi to take me out to Balthazar Pottage's island.

I found I enjoyed the brisk walk in the cold air despite the chilly crossing. The house that matched the address I'd been given was decorated with red, white, and green lights that danced to the beat of Christmas music. This somehow made me relax just a bit. The woman couldn't be too intense if she lived in such a whimsically decorated home.

"Mrs. Cribbage," I said when a woman with a friendly smile opened the door.

"Call me Edith. And you must be Cait. Please do come in."

I followed the woman into the small but neat home. She offered me a seat on the sofa, gave me a cup of tea, and presented a tray of delicious-looking pastries. I could sense by her welcoming smile that she was a gracious hostess who was comfortable in most social situations.

"You wanted to ask me about Charles Pottage's kidnapping?" she began.

"Yes. I'm looking into it for Mr. Pottage." I explained about the apartments and the deal we'd made.

"I'm happy to help if I can, but I have to confess I slept through the whole thing. I've tortured myself about that fact every day since it occurred. I don't understand how I could have slept so soundly. Sure I was tired, but not that tired."

"Can you tell me everything that happened that day?"

"I can try." The woman adjusted her position in her chair so she faced me directly. "Mr. and Mrs. Pottage were fighting and I think that upset Charles. I realize he was only six weeks old, but babies can pick up on these things, and I'm afraid their tension made him tense. Anyway, Charles had been extra fussy ever since the mister returned from his business trip."

"And when was that?"

"The day before the christening. I'm afraid Mrs. Pottage had arranged the whole thing without telling him what she was doing, and he wasn't happy about that."

"Okay. Go on."

"Mrs. Pottage was busy that day, getting ready for her guests, so I took charge of getting Charles ready. I remember how adorable he looked as I dressed him in the long white gown she had given me for the occasion. He looked like a little angel. He really was such a precious child. All of the children I cared for over the years were precious to me, but he touched my heart in a special way."

I noticed the woman had teared up just a bit. I felt bad that I was putting her through what had to have been a horrible memory.

"Were there other guests upstairs while you were getting the baby ready for the ceremony?" I asked.

"No. It was just Charles and me in the nursery and Mr. and Mrs. Pottage in the master suite. There were guests staying at the residence, but Mr. Pottage insisted that they be given rooms downstairs. He brought one of the gatehouse guards in to make certain no one came up to the second story. It seemed as if he was concerned that the baby might be in some sort of danger. I thought the extra guard was silly and unnecessary at the time, but now I can see that the man was wise to be diligent in his attempt to protect his family. In the end I guess it didn't really matter."

"What happened after you got Charles dressed?"

"Mrs. Pottage came to fetch Charles just prior to the start of the ceremony. I wanted to attend the baptism, but she could tell I was tired, so she insisted that I have a nap while I could. It was sweet of her to be so concerned about me. She even had a cup of tea sent up for me, even though she had guests to attend to."

I frowned. "Tea? I spoke to the guard who'd been at the stairs and he told me no one was on the second story other than Mrs. Pottage. Who brought you the tea?"

"No one. Mrs. Pottage had the kitchen send it up via the dumbwaiter. I drank the tea and fell asleep, and the next thing I knew, the missus was screaming that Charles was missing from his crib. It was my job to look after the baby, but I never even woke up. I still can't believe I didn't see or hear anything. I've been devastated by that fact ever since I let some monster whisk poor Charles away."

Suddenly I knew exactly what had happened.

I was a bundle of nerves the entire trip out to Pottage's island. The man wasn't going to be happy to hear what I had to tell him. I just hoped he wasn't so mad as to call off our deal. For the first time since this whole thing began things were starting to make sense.

I felt a sense of dread as I walked from the dock to the house. The information I had to share with the man wasn't going to be easy to hear and I hated to be the one to have to tell him.

"You're late," Balthazar Pottage snapped when he opened the door after my quick knock.

"If you had a phone I could have called to let you know I had an interview on San Juan Island," I snapped back.

He looked surprised by my sharp reply. "I never said I didn't have a phone."

I supposed that much was true. When I'd asked to use his phone the first time I'd visited the island he simply hadn't answered.

"I'm sorry I'm late, but I have news. If you'll let me in we can get started."

I followed the old man down the hallway to the same room we'd sat in on the other times I'd been in his home. He had a fire going in the stone fireplace, but there was a definite chill in the room. I rubbed my hands together to warm them.

"You said you have news?" Pottage asked.

"I do."

"You found my son?"

"No. Not yet, but I'm pretty sure I know what happened to him." I sat down in the chair next to the one he was sitting in. "I'm afraid it was your wife who kidnapped your son."

Pottage frowned. "What kind of nonsense is this? Are you trying to fool an old man out of an apartment building?"

"Just hear me out," I began.

"Very well," the man said gruffly, "but stick to the facts. I don't need you trying to confuse me with a lot of meaningless banter."

"I will." I leaned forward in my chair. "Based on what I've learned, you and Belle weren't getting along at the time your son was kidnapped."

He sighed. "That much I am afraid is true. I was away at work quite a lot and Belle got lonely alone on the island. I suppose I should have looked at the situation from her perspective, but I didn't. All I could see were my own needs and the needs of the business I had spent my life building."

"So she wanted you to spend more time on the island?"

"No, she wanted to spend more time with me in Seattle. She said she was bored on the island, but I refused to even consider her request to get out more often."

"Why?"

"I was frightened. I was a lot older than she was and I was afraid she'd meet someone younger and leave me. I realize she could have met someone on the island, but she was attracted to wealthy men in positions of power, so I thought it was less likely she'd meet the man of her dreams on Madrona Island."

"The man of her dreams? That sounds like you believed she was shopping around. Did she ever give you any indication that she wanted to leave you?"

"Not at first. I'm afraid it was my need to isolate her that drove her away. She came to me just before she found out she was pregnant and told me she planned to leave me. I begged her to stay. I promised

I would give her the freedom she longed for. She said she'd think about it, and while she was thinking she realized she was pregnant and agreed to stay for the baby's sake."

"And yet it seems you tightened your control over Belle even more after she decided to stay."

He dropped his head. "I did. But for a different reason than you might assume. A few months before Charles was born I received some very specific threats from a man I had evicted from his home. I was afraid he might hurt Belle in order to get even with me, so I hired a couple of men to guard the front gate. I was afraid my enemies would get to me through my wife, so I refused to allow her to leave the property. She wasn't at all happy about that. She suspected I was just the same jealous man I'd always been. She called me her jailer, but all I really wanted to do was protect her."

I leaned forward. "And after Charles was born?"

"I became even more neurotic about protecting my wife and child. Looking back, I can see that I suffocated her. I didn't allow her to leave the estate and I didn't allow anyone to visit. Not even her family."

"So she arranged the christening without your consent," I continued.

"Yes. I went away on a business trip and was furious with her when I got home and realized what she had done. We fought."

I paused for a moment and gathered my thoughts. I didn't want to sound judgmental, but I couldn't help myself. "I understand you were trying to protect your wife from a danger I imagine was very real to you, but I'm sure from her perspective you seemed more interested in controlling her than protecting her. She probably realized that the only way to regain her freedom was to leave you once and for all. Of course she now had the baby to consider, and I think she knew you'd never allow her to take Charles with her."

An angry look came over his face. "Damn right I would never have allowed her to take my son from me."

"It seems you left her no choice," I said as gently as I could.

"What do you mean, no choice?"

"In her mind, I suspect she felt the only way out of her loveless marriage and barren life was to kidnap her own son."

"What nonsense are you suggesting?"

"Think about it," I insisted. "She wanted to leave, but she knew you would never allow her to take Charles. She realized that the only way you'd let her go was if you believed she was leaving alone."

Pottage frowned. "How is it even possible that Belle kidnapped Charles? I kept my eye on the stairs the entire evening and the windows were covered with bars."

I grimaced. No wonder Belle wanted to leave. It sounded like she'd lived in a prison.

"I believe Belle sent Charles down to the kitchen via the dumbwaiter. The nanny told me that your wife sent tea up to her through the dumbwaiter and that she fell asleep after she drank it. She must have been drugged. I believe that when Belle went upstairs to check on Charles the first time she sent him down the dumbwaiter to someone who was waiting below."

"Who?"

"I don't know."

"But the house was searched from top to bottom, as were the vehicles of the guests before they were allowed to leave."

"I still haven't figured out who Belle's accomplice was, or how they removed Charles from the property, but the dumbwaiter scenario is the only one that makes sense."

The old man sighed. "I have to admit that your theory does seem to hold water. That boy was everything to me. He still is. Can you find him?"

"I can try."

I thought about it all the way home. Someone had to have managed to get the baby off the estate and past the guard, but who? One of the other staff members? Belle's sister or best friend? Surely not one of the locals she had invited to the christening.

When I got back on Madrona Island I decided to pay an overdue visit to Tripp Brimmer. He'd been the deputy who had originally responded to the call about the baby's disappearance and I'd never gotten around to speaking to him. Luckily, he was in when I arrived at his home. I felt like there was a single piece of the puzzle that was eluding me and hoped the man who had spent hours trying to solve the case could help me.

The first thing I did was share with him my theory about the dumbwaiter.

"That's brilliant. I can't believe I didn't think of it. It makes perfect sense."

"I just happened to stumble across the right information at the right time," I commented, even though I did feel the dumbwaiter should have occurred to him during the initial investigation. "What I'm trying to figure out is who the accomplice was."

Tripp frowned. "I can't imagine. When I heard about the kidnapping I called in all my backup personnel. We interviewed every person on the premises and searched the entire house. We also searched every vehicle. That baby had simply disappeared."

"So whoever was helping Belle must have got the baby off the property before you arrived."

"There was no way that baby was still on the property when I got there. There was no way I could have overlooked him. We searched every inch of the place. Every person I spoke to confirmed that not a single person left the premises between the time Mrs. Pottage first checked on her son and when she found him missing a short while later."

"Yes, but if Belle is the person who arranged for the baby to disappear, perhaps he was already gone. Maybe she sent him down the dumbwaiter when she initially went upstairs to put him to bed. Maybe she lied when she reported back that he was sleeping peacefully a short while later."

"Of course." Tripp shook his head. "I should have thought of that. It was brilliant really. We never considered any of the people who left the estate before Belle went to check on the baby the first time as suspects because we believed he was seen sleeping in his crib after they'd left."

"Belle did seem to have the whole thing planned out," I commented.

Tripp got up from the table. He walked down the hall to a room I assumed was an office. He came back with a file folder and opened it. It looked as if he still had a copy of the report he'd filed twenty years earlier.

"It says here," he began, "that only Father Kilian and the mayor and his wife left the estate prior to the first time Mrs. Pottage went in to check on the baby. I don't really see either of them kidnapping a child in spite of the fact that it seemed Mrs. Pottage had a good reason to want to do so."

"What about the caterer?" I asked.

Tripp looked at his notes and frowned. "What caterer? I have in my notes that the family cook was taking care of the buffet lunch and she was still there when I arrived."

"I found out that another woman brought the food and then left. Father Kilian saw her loading her van when he left and others reported that she left shortly after the ceremony to attend another event."

"No caterer was mentioned when I interviewed everyone at the time of the kidnapping."

"I think she must have stayed behind the scenes because none of the local guests mentioned seeing her, although the staff seems to have been aware of her presence. They may not have mentioned her because she left early and was only at the estate for a short time after the ceremony concluded."

"Do you have a name?" Tripp asked.

"No. No one, it seems, knows who she was. I didn't think to ask Balthazar Pottage if he knew the woman's name. I guess I'll need to go back to the island."

"You're busy and I'm retired. I'll go over there tomorrow to ask him about it. I'll call you either way. If we can get a name maybe we can track her down."

Chapter 13

Tara and I had missed one of our favorite television shows, *Cooking with Cathy*, for the past couple of weeks due to conflicts in our schedules. But tonight was the Christmas special, and we both found ourselves with open evenings. The doctor wanted to keep Destiny in the hospital overnight because her blood pressure was a little high, and Cody had called to say he had several stories to write for the paper's midweek edition and was going to stay in the office to write them, which meant that Tara and I were both free to spend the evening as we chose.

"I've really missed this," Tara commented as she measured the flour for a batch of cookies. We'd already made flavored fudge, white house cookies, and twistree bread. We were working on the sugar cookies and planned to make Kolachy and almond rocco next.

"Me too. It seems like we've both been really busy lately. It's nice to have some best friend time. Did you grab the sugar?"

"Not yet."

"Have you talked to Destiny about the baby?" I asked.

"Actually, I have. She's going to keep the baby after all. She told me she knew once she held him that she couldn't give him away."

"I'm not surprised," I said as I began measuring the wet ingredients for the cookies. "Has she decided what to do about school? She's such a bright girl. It would be a shame if she wasn't able to get a good education."

"She has that all worked out," Tara informed me. "Sister Mary is going to help her graduate high school a year early, at the end of this school year, and then Destiny plans to move in with her aunt, who lives near Oregon State. The aunt is retired and has agreed to watch James while Destiny takes classes."

"That's awesome. Is she going to continue to live with you until she leaves for college?"

"Yes, it looks like she will. She's shared her plan with her mother, who now supports her decision to keep the baby, but she told me that she'd still prefer to stay with me. It'll be fun to have a baby in the house."

I began to assemble the ingredients for the glazed pecans.

"I'm really going to miss them when they leave," Tara added. "I got to hold the baby today when I went to visit Destiny in the hospital. I can't wait to have one of my own."

"Really?" I frowned. "It seems like everyone's biological clock is ticking but mine."

"What do you mean by that?" Tara asked as she spooned the dough onto the cookie sheet.

"Cody mentioned the other night that he was beginning to think about having a family. Now you're telling me that you can't wait to have children. I just don't feel like I'm ready."

"Why not? You're great with kids," Tara pointed out.

"Yeah, but I'm not sure I'm ready to have them all the time. I'm so busy as it is. There's no way I'd have time for a baby."

"Maybe not." Tara slid the cookie sheet into the oven. "But it seems to me that there comes a time in a relationship when you have to figure out if you're on the same page as the person you're involved with. If Cody is ready for children and you aren't, that could eventually become an issue."

"I guess you might have a point. We haven't been together all that long, though. I can't imagine it will be an issue for quite some time."

"Perhaps. But maybe you should start to really think about the situation if it does come up."

"Yeah, I suppose. I bet those orange scones would be a hit at the store."

"We should try them out after Christmas."

I really didn't want to think about having to ask hard questions in my relationship with Cody. Tara might have a point, but I didn't think Cody and I were anywhere near that yet. Still, I supposed we would get to that place sooner or later; maybe it wasn't a bad idea to try to figure out where I stood on issues such as marriage and children. But not tonight. Tonight I just wanted to bake with my best friend and enjoy the warmth of my little cabin on a cold, blustery night.

I'd planned to go to bed after Tara left but found I was unable to get to sleep, so I poured myself a glass of wine and sat down on the sofa with Max and Ebenezer for company. I felt like I was close to tracking down Charles. I just hoped Pottage knew the name of the caterer and we were able to use that information to track her down. It would be a shame to come this far and not be able to reunite the old man with his son.

Of course the possibility existed that the boy was dead. I only assumed the woman who'd helped Belle take him away either raised him herself after Belle died or found another family to do so. I supposed the reason she didn't return him to his father after his mother's death was because something had happened to the child along the way.

And if she did raise the child, I had to wonder how the boy who was now a man would take the news that the woman who'd raised him was actually the person who'd helped his mother take him from his father. Would he even want to see Pottage?

All good questions, but not really answerable at that point.

"So what do you think, kitty?" I asked Ebenezer. "Are you ready to help out? I've enjoyed your company, but it seems like it might be time to pitch in and get this case solved."

Ebenezer just stared at me. He lay his head on my lap and began to purr. It appeared he wasn't quite as motivated as I was to get things wrapped up.

I petted the cat as I watched the flames from the fire. I wished I'd thought to ask Balthazar Pottage about the woman who'd catered the event. I found that not knowing was making me nuts. Perhaps the woman's name had been mentioned on one of the documents in the box he'd given me. I got up from the sofa and went over to the counter, where the box and envelope were sitting. I had casually searched things, but I hadn't taken the time to look at every newspaper article or read every document. If nothing else, maybe looking through all the paperwork would be boring enough to put me to sleep. I brought everything back to the sofa with me.

The articles consisted of retellings of the day of the kidnapping and the subsequent search for the child. There were photos of the baby, along with a plea from Belle to please find her child and bring him home. He was an infant when he was taken and it was winter and cold, so in most of the photos the baby was swaddled in blankets, his features hard to discern.

I couldn't imagine how hard the loss of his son must have been for Pottage. Belle had had the luxury of knowing the baby was alive and being cared for, but as far as her husband knew, his son was in the hands of a monster. No wonder he'd turned into a reclusive old man.

I sorted through the articles and photographs, looking for any sort of clue, no matter how minor. The couple had been photographed from several different angles during the christening of their son. The baby was unswaddled as Father Kilian poured water over his forehead. I frowned as I held the photo up to a better light. Could it really be that easy?

Chapter 14

Tuesday, December 22

"I know the line is long and everyone is anxious to see Santa," Tara announced, "but I really need everyone to wait patiently."

The Santa idea had been so popular that Tara had extended the hours to run through Christmas Eve. Alex seemed happy in his role and the mothers who browsed through the store while their children were in line seemed more than willing to repay our efforts by buying our coffee, books, and novelty items.

Tara was thrilled that we'd made enough money to cover expenses for the next few months, which we feared would be slow, so the general atmosphere in the shop was barely suppressed euphoria.

"Why don't you pass out candy canes to all the kids after they've had a chance to sit on Santa's lap?" Tara suggested.

"I'm on it." Passing out candy seemed a mindless enough activity, which was perfect for me because my mind was completely occupied by Tripp and the final piece of the puzzle, which I hoped he'd bring back from his meeting with Balthazar Pottage. When I'd first taken on this quest I hadn't really believed I had a chance of actually solving the twenty-year-old kidnapping case, but if my hunch proved to be correct I would have done just that.

I looked at Ebenezer, who was lounging in a basket next to Santa's chair. I hadn't thought he'd helped much, but it turned out that he'd brought me the most important clue of all.

"Do you work here?" a woman in a blue coat asked.

"Yes."

"Can you explain how the cat adoption works?"

"Sure."

"How about the kitty next to Santa? Is he available?"

"No, I'm sorry, he isn't. But we have some great cats next door in the lounge. Just let me hand off my candy chore to someone else and I'll explain everything to you."

It turned out that the woman was very interested in adopting not one but two cats. She filled out an application and I promised to hang on to the cats she'd picked out until I could process her paperwork. She agreed to come back the following day. It looked like two of my little darlings were going to have homes for Christmas if everything checked out.

I was on my way back to the coffee bar side of the bookstore to help out with the crowd when Tripp texted me. He had a name for the woman who had catered the party. I gasped when I found out my hunch had been correct. It looked like I'd found Charles Pottage. Now I just needed to inform Santa as to his true identity.

"You have to be kidding me," Alex said later that evening, after everyone had left and the store had closed. "You expect me to believe that I'm this Charles Pottage you've been looking for?"

"I know it seems unbelievable, but consider the evidence. According to Balthazar, the woman who catered the baptism and we assume helped Belle Pottage to remove the baby from the property was named Lucy Turner. Your name is Alex Turner and you mentioned earlier that your mother's name was Lucy."

"Lucy Turner isn't an uncommon name," Alex pointed out.

"True, but then there's your birthmark." I handed Alex the photo of the christening. "I noticed Charles had a birthmark in the exact shape and general area as you do when I saw this photo. Tripp confirmed with Balthazar Pottage that his son had a heart-shaped birthmark on his forehead."

"But I'm not adopted. I can't be this Charles," Alex argued.

"Perhaps, but we would still like to speak to your mother."

"My mother is dead. I told you that the first day we met."

That was true. He *had* told us that his mother had passed away.

"Is there anyone your mother was close to? Anyone with whom she might have shared the truth?" I asked.

Alex ran his hand through his thick hair. He sighed. "Yeah. She might have told her sister Grace. Grace still lives here on the island. In fact, I've been staying with her. I can arrange a meeting, but only to prove to you that you're wrong."

"Thank you." I placed my hand on Alex's arm, but he shook it off. "I'd appreciate that."

After we locked up Tara went home to relieve Cassie, who was staying with Destiny, and I went with Alex to his aunt's. I promised to stop by Tara's later to fill her in on the outcome of the conversation. I just hoped Lucy had told Grace what had happened twenty years ago, and that Grace would be willing to share that information with Alex and me. If not, I wasn't sure how I'd ever prove Alex was Charles

Pottage. A DNA test, I guessed. But Alex had been so great, I'd hate to force the issue.

When I walked into the house with Alex I could tell his aunt knew who I was and why I was there. She offered me a cup of coffee, but I could see how nervous she was.

"I guess you figured things out," she started.

"So it's true?" Alex spat.

"I'm afraid so. I've wanted to tell you a million times, but your mother insisted that I keep her secret. She loved you and I loved her, so I did as she asked, but I never felt right about it."

"My mother kidnapped me?" Alex appeared to be in shock.

"That wasn't the way it was," Grace defended her sister. "Please let me explain."

Alex didn't say anything, but he didn't walk out either.

"Your mama met Mrs. Pottage when she was called in to sub for the regular maid. Lucy was sad and lonely after her fiancé died unexpectedly, and Mrs. Pottage—Belle—was sad and lonely too, because she was stuck in a marriage to a man she didn't love. They forged a bond, I'm guessing, based on their loneliness, during the week your mama cleaned the house. They became friends. Secret friends, although I wasn't certain at the time why they kept their friendship to themselves."

Alex appeared to still be listening.

"Belle wanted to leave her overprotective husband, to divorce him and start again fresh, but she knew he'd never allow her to take you with her. I don't believe Balthazar Pottage loved Belle the way he should have, but he seemed to love you."

Grace twisted a Kleenex as she spoke. It was obvious this was difficult for her.

"I wasn't privy to all the details, but it seemed Belle spent a lot of time trying to figure out how to liberate both of you from this very rich and powerful man. She came up with the idea of pretending you'd been kidnapped. She thought once your father realized you weren't going to be found, she could convince him to give her a divorce. Somehow she talked Lucy into helping her. Belle planned the christening party as a diversion. Then she used the isolation her domineering husband had insisted on to her advantage. She made a fuss about taking you upstairs for a nap. She drugged the nanny and then lowered you down to Lucy in the dumbwaiter. Lucy simply hid you in her van and left. A good half hour after Lucy left the property, Belle went back upstairs and told everyone you were sleeping peacefully. Lucy was on a boat heading east before anyone knew you were missing."

"This whole thing is crazy," Alex said eventually.

"Maybe, but I think your mother—your real mother—felt desperate. Desperate people do desperate things."

"And the accident that killed Belle? Was that really an accident?" Alex asked.

"Yes, I believe it was. Belle had planned to wait until after the new year before announcing that she was going to visit a friend and then simply disappear with you. It was Lucy's opinion that something happened to move up her timetable. Unfortunately, she used bad judgment when she attempted to drive on icy roads."

Alex got up and began pacing around the room. Not that I blamed him; this was a lot to take in. To be told that your whole life had been a lie must be incomprehensible. I felt bad for him, but there was nothing I could do to make him feel better about the situation.

"So why didn't my mother—I mean Lucy—take me to my father after Belle died?" Alex finally asked.

"I wanted her to. I begged her to. At first she insisted that if she brought you back everyone would realize her part in the faked kidnapping and she might end up spending the rest of her life in prison. I tried to convince her to drop you off at the church or a shelter with a note stating who you were, but she refused. In order to get Lucy to go along with her plan Belle had pretty much convinced her that Balthazar Pottage was a monster. While I don't think he would have won any husband-of-the-year awards, I don't think he was quite as bad as Belle made him out to be."

Alex ran his hands through his hair and then sat back down on the sofa. He looked directly at his aunt. "If my mother was unwilling to tell the truth, why didn't you?"

"I told you: Lucy was my sister and I loved her. She loved you. You were good for her. You helped to mend her broken heart, so I turned a blind eye and prayed that God would forgive me for the secret I kept. I'm truly sorry." There were tears streaming down the woman's face. "I hope you can forgive me."

Alex tilted his head so that he was looking at the ceiling. "I don't know at this point what I am or am not willing to do, or who I am or am not willing to forgive. I need time to process all this."

He got up from the sofa and slipped on his coat. Then he looked at me. "Don't worry; I'll show up for my shift as Santa tomorrow."

With that he was gone.

Chapter 15

Wednesday, December 23

The church was packed as nervous parents waited for the Christmas play to begin. The rehearsals had gone smoothly, so I wasn't sure why I was so nervous. I supposed my jitters had more to do with my anxiety over the outcome of the conversation going on down the hall than with the success of the play. Balthazar Pottage had come to Madrona Island after I'd visited him to explain everything I had discovered. He was hurt by what Belle had done to him, but he very much wanted to meet his son. Alex was hesitant at first, but eventually he'd agreed to speak to his father, with Father Kilian acting as a go-between.

Cody came up behind me as I peeked around the curtain at the crowd. "It looks like we have a full house."

"Yeah, it's a good turnout. I'm glad. The kids worked hard."

My voice sounded flat to my own ears, but that was the most enthusiasm I could muster.

"It's going to be okay, you know," Cody said into my ear.

"I know. The kids are ready. It'll be great."

"That's not what I meant," he corrected me. "I know this whole thing has been a shock to both Alex and Balthazar Pottage, but my gut tells me they'll get past what happened years ago and develop some sort of a relationship. It may not be what they would have had if Alex had grown up as Charles, but I could tell by the look on both their faces that they want things to work out between them."

"I hope so," I said, even though I was less certain than Cody sounded. "It doesn't seem right that they wasted so many years apart. Although," I added, "if Alex had grown up as Charles and Pottage had treated him the way he treated Belle, they might hate each other by now. At least they have a chance of establishing a relationship from a more mature perspective on both their parts. When I spoke to Pottage this afternoon I could tell he was a different man from the one I met that first day. He's going to do as he promised with the apartment building, and he mentioned a couple of other wrongs he wanted to right before it was too late."

"Ms. Cait, I think I might throw up," Holly said from behind where Cody and I were standing.

"Are you nervous?" I asked as I turned around to look at the girl.

"Terrified."

"Try to ignore the audience," I suggested. "You did great in the dress rehearsal."

"I can't ignore the audience. My parents and grandparents and aunts and uncles and cousins are all out there. Not to mention my big brother, who will torture me for life if I mess up. Maybe someone else can do my part. I really think I might pass out."

Cody took Holly by the shoulders and turned her so that she was facing him. "I used to get stage fright when I was younger too," he informed her.

"You did?"

"I absolutely did. I even threw up on my teacher's shoe during my first-grade talent show, but then I learned a trick."

"What trick?"

"Find someone in the audience you trust and look at that person and only that person."

"I trust you."

"Okay, here's what we're going to do. I'm going to go out into the audience and sit in the front row. When it's your turn to say your lines I want you to look at me and only me. Can you do that?"

Holly took a deep breath. "Yeah, I think I can."

"Great. Now hurry back and slip into your costume. I'll be right behind you. I want to talk to everyone before we begin."

"You really do have a way with kids," I said to Cody.

He shrugged. "I like them. They know it and generally trust me. You're pretty good with them too, you know."

"Maybe, but I don't have the knack for smoothing things over the way you do. You're going to be a fantastic dad one day."

Cody smiled.

"Did Destiny show up with James?"

At Trinity's insistence, Destiny had agreed to let James play the part of Baby Jesus. She was going to place him in the manger while the curtain was closed between scenes because she didn't want anyone other than her carrying him.

"Yeah, she's here," Cody answered. "She assured me that he'd been fed and changed and will most likely sleep through the whole thing. She's going to be waiting just offstage just in case."

"She certainly has taken to this mothering thing," I commented.

"Yeah, she really has. I think Destiny and James are going to be just fine."

"I hope so."

"By the way," Cody informed me, "the guest list for tomorrow is up to twenty."

"Twenty?"

"I guess word has gotten out that we're having a Christmas Eve party. I hate to turn anyone away. Everyone who has asked to come would have been alone otherwise."

"That's fine," I assured Cody. "I'll just make a few additional appetizers. Maybe some sausage bread. Everyone loves that. How's Mr. Parsons with the increase in the guest list?"

"He's fine," Cody said. "He tends to be a bit of a loner, with only a few close friends, but he seems downright excited about having a big shindig in his house this year. He even asked me to take him into town to buy new clothes to wear. I really think he's enjoying all the attention."

"That's good."

"Mr. Cody," one of the cast members called out. "We're ready for the power circle."

"Okay. I'm on my way," he said, then looked at me for a moment.

"Go ahead. I'll be along in a minute."

I continued to watch the crowd after Cody had gone. I hadn't seen Father Kilian come in yet, which most likely meant Pottage and Alex were still talking. I hoped Father Kilian would convince them both to attend the play.

"Good turnout," Tara said from behind me.

"Yeah. I hope the kids don't freak out when they see how many people are out there."

"They'll be fine," Tara insisted. "The worst part of performing is the anxiety beforehand. I'm sure that once the play gets going they'll forget all about the audience."

"I hope so."

"All the kids in the play sing in the choir. They're used to performing in front of a crowd."

"That's true."

"Are you coming back to the choir room for Cody's talk?" Tara asked.

"Yeah," I said, though I continued to look out around the curtain. "I was watching for Father Kilian. I wanted to ask him how it went before the play got underway, but I haven't seen him."

"I'm sure you can catch him later," Tara commented as she walked over and stood beside me.

"Yeah, you're right."

I was about to drop the drape and head toward the choir room, where Cody and Sister Mary were helping the kids with their costumes, when Tara stopped me.

"Look who just walked into the room."

I turned back to the audience and watched as Alex came in with Balthazar Pottage and Father Kilian. All three men took seats near the back. I had to smile as I realized that maybe we had the Christmas miracle I'd been praying for.

Chapter 16

December 24

"How's the corn bread coming for the chicken and corn bread?" I asked Tara.

"Almost done."

I'd assumed she would be spending Christmas Eve with Destiny and her family, but she'd informed me that the Paulsons had a houseful of relatives who had come to see the baby, so she'd just as soon attend the party at Mr. Parsons's. Danny had decided to come as well, which led to Aiden and his girlfriend, Siobhan and Finn, and Cassie and my mother as additional guests. At last count the old ballroom was set up with tables to accommodate thirty.

Mr. Parsons seemed delighted. I was pretty sure that ballroom hadn't been used in his lifetime. Fortunately, Tara, Danny, Finn, and Siobhan had all come over to help me cook and clean in preparation for what was quickly becoming the event of the season.

I would have enjoyed spending a quiet evening with Cody, but in spite of the fact that I was going to be exhausted by the time the party was over, I found myself pulled into the energy created when friends come together to share a special occasion. I was particularly thrilled when Balthazar Pottage agreed to attend with Alex and his aunt. Not only had Pottage donated a precooked ham and two precooked turkeys but he'd had a delivery service bring fresh flowers that must have cost a fortune at this time of year and boxes of candy to share.

"I saw you chatting with Mr. Pottage earlier," Tara commented. "He must be pretty pleased with the way things turned out."

"He's ecstatic. He pulled me aside when he first got here and handed me a signed and notarized contract that states he'll repair the apartment building and then gift it to the tenants, just like he promised."

"I bet his attorney was thrilled to have to do that on Christmas Eve."

"He probably wasn't happy about it, but I have a feeling Pottage is one of his best clients. As far as I'm concerned, it could have waited until after the new year, but I think he wanted our agreement all wrapped up."

I began peeling potatoes to go with the turkey.

"Do you think Alex and his father will stay in touch?" Tara asked.

"I think they will. Alex mentioned that Pottage plans to have the old house on the island renovated for Alex to stay in whenever he's here."

"That house is huge."

"I think Pottage is hoping Alex will eventually move to the island and give him grandbabies to dote on."

I sliced the potatoes and slid them into boiling water, then turned my attention to the fresh vegetables that needed to be washed and trimmed for cooking. I could hear the music from the stereo Cody had set up in the other room. There was something sort of perfect about Christmas carols on a snowy night. Danny had built a fire in the ballroom fireplace and Siobhan had lit about a hundred scented candles. It was going to be a magical evening.

"Is Ebenezer still with you?" Tara asked.

"Yeah, he's at the cabin. I'm going to keep him until Pottage goes back to his island. He rented a room in town and plans to stay until after Alex returns to college so they can spend as much time together as possible."

"That's nice. Of course I kind of think we won't have the benefit of Alex's help next summer, as we'd hoped. Now that he's heir to the Pottage millions I doubt he'll be willing to work in a bookstore."

Tara had a point, but I was so happy for both Alex and Balthazar Pottage that I didn't care.

"Do you have any more of those stuffed mushrooms?" Cassie asked as she stepped into the kitchen. "They were a huge hit."

"There are a couple of trays on the back counter," Tara informed her. "How's it going out there?"

"Good. Everyone is having a wonderful time. Cody wanted me to tell you that he and Finn went over to Francine's to get some more folding chairs for the group from the church."

"The group from the church?" I asked.

"Yeah, they came with Father Kilian. They were at the Christmas Eve service, and when Father Kilian found out they were going to be alone he called Cody to ask if we had room for a few more. Cody told him the more the merrier and then grabbed Finn to go for more chairs. I hope we have enough food."

"We'll have enough," Tara assured her. "If it looks like we're going to run short we'll just have Father Kilian pray over it."

"I think we might already have had our Christmas miracle," I pointed out

"There's always room for another miracle," Tara reminded me.

"Let me help you with that," I said to Cassie as she tried to juggle two trays of mushrooms and open the door.

I couldn't help but feel a warmth in my heart as I walked through Mr. Parsons's normally cold and empty house, which was now warm and filled with friends and neighbors. Mr. Parsons was smiling. Balthazar Pottage was smiling. The old mansion was truly filled with the love and joy of the season.

"I'm exhausted," Cody said to me later that night, after we'd served over forty dinners. Fortunately, Tara, Siobhan, Finn, and Danny had stayed to help us clean up.

"Me too, but it was nice."

"Very nice."

"I heard Mr. Parsons say something about making it an annual tradition."

"At least we have a year to plan the next one," Cody commented.

We were curled up in my bed looking out the large window in my loft bedroom, which was framed in small red and green lights. Cody had his arm around me and we were propped up with extra pillows so that we could look out at the moon shining down on the glassy ocean. It had snowed off and on for most of the evening, but the clouds had parted to reveal a full moon just as we arrived back at the cabin.

"Did you hear that Pottage plans to fix up the old estate for Alex?" I asked.

"Mr. Parsons mentioned something about it. I guess he spoke to him about it this evening. He thinks it will be a good place for Alex to raise a family."

"It would be an awesome place. It's a huge estate right on the water. Any kid would be lucky to grow up there."

"I guess his plan got Mr. Parsons to thinking," Cody shared.

"Hmm" I murmured. I felt myself begin to drift off as I relaxed to the sound of Cody's heart beating under my ear as my head rested on his chest.

"Mr. Parsons wants to leave me his house. He thinks it will make a wonderful place for the two of us to raise a family."

Suddenly I was wide awake. I leaned up on one elbow and looked at Cody.

"He wants to leave you his house?" I clarified.

"He's getting on in years and he doesn't have a family. He told me that I'm the closest thing he's ever had to a family and he very much wants to leave me the house and the land it sits on. I think he's assuming, based on our current relationship, that it's only a matter of time before the two of us fill the empty rooms with children of our own. So what do you think?"

I hesitated. "About the house or the children?"

"Both, actually."

What did I think? I might not quite be ready to settle down and have kids, but I did love Cody and I did see us with a house full of offspring one day. Mr. Parsons's house was not only huge but it was on a large piece of land right on the water. And best of all, the house was right next door to my Aunt Maggie.

I looked at Cody. He actually looked nervous about my answer.

I grinned. "I think Mr. Parsons is a very generous man and I would very much like to fill those rooms with little Wests one day."

Cody smiled. "Really?"

"Really."

Cody sat up just a bit. He reached into the drawer in the bed stand where he'd stashed his wallet and keys. He pulled out a small box, which he handed to me. "Merry Christmas."

I looked at the box. "I said *someday*."

"Don't worry, it isn't a ring. I know you aren't ready for that and I'm willing to wait. It's your Christmas gift. I was going to save it for the morning, but I want you to have it now."

I opened the box and inside was a delicate necklace on a silver chain. It had two small hearts, entwined with a stone in the center of each.

"Our birthstones," Cody informed me. "Ruby for me and emerald for you. I thought it fortunate that we were born in months that are represented by one red stone and one green. Very Christmassy."

"It's beautiful. Thank you so much."

Cody took the necklace from the box and slipped it around my neck. His fingers sent chills down my spine as he fastened it.

"I'm afraid with all the investigating and last-minute dinner parties I never did get you a gift," I confessed. "To be honest, I had no idea what you'd want."

"I have a suggestion," Cody whispered in my ear.

I smiled and snuggled back down under the covers. There was no doubt about it. We were going to be very late indeed to my mother's in the morning.

USA Today best-selling author Kathi Daley lives in beautiful Lake Tahoe with her husband Ken. When she isn't writing, she likes spending time hiking the miles of desolate trails surrounding her home. Find out more about her books at www.kathidaley.com

Made in the USA
Las Vegas, NV
21 August 2023

76402481R00105